'Fresh, funny, fabulous, Yes Yes More More had me gripped. These stories surprise and delight. Anna Wood is the real thing – a writer you immediately want more of.'

JACKIE KAY

'Yes Yes More More gives us precisely realised worlds of gloriously observant and hyper-attentive specificity. Devoid of cliche, Anna Wood's writing presents people and situations that are laugh-out-loud funny but there is a stealth to her stories, an unshowy intelligence, which makes them deeply satisfying.'

WENDY ERSKINE

'Vivid, heartbreaking and jubilant – I couldn't get enough of Yes Yes More More. Anna Wood examines life under a brilliant shifting light, finding beauty, horror and meaning in every moment. A triumph.'

CATRIONA WARD

'Bursting with zing and vitality, Yes Yes More More is an absolute marvel of a short story collection. What it feels like to be alive, to dance wildly, to be surrounded by friends.'

ELIZABETH MACNEAL

'Anna Wood's stories are urban, sexy, darkly and uniquely comic, and tuned to the zeitgeist like the bass player every band would want. Her prose has the precision and economy of the best poetry, deployed to offer us cinematic glimpses of the lives we recognise, endure and rejoice in. Fiction has a new star in its firmament.'

CAROL ANN DUFFY

T0167999

THE

INDIGO

PRESS

YES YES
MORE MORE

YES YES
MORE MORE

ANNA WOOD

THE

INDIGO

PRESS

THE INDIGO PRESS
50 Albemarle Street
London W1S 4BD
www.theindigopress.com

The Indigo Press Publishing Limited Reg. No. 10995574
Registered Office: Wellesley House, Duke of Wellington Avenue
Royal Arsenal, London SE18 6SS

First published in Great Britain in 2021 by The Indigo Press

A CIP catalogue record for this book is available from the British Library

ISBN: 978-1-911648-28-4
eBook ISBN: 978-1-911648-29-1

Design by houseofthought.io
Typeset in Goudy Old Style by Tetragon, London
Printed and bound in Great Britain by TJ Books Limited, Padstow

MIX
Paper from
responsible sources
FSC® C013056
www.fsc.org

For my friends

CONTENTS

Rise Up Singing

You do get hot summers in Bolton and we had one that year, for weeks on end as I remember it although it may just have been a fortnight or so. This was 1990, I think, and it was a Friday afternoon because we had double English with Mr Howard. Lisa and Claire had both taken a full tab, but Janey and I just had half each.

"Who or what do you think is causing the friction between Jane and Elizabeth?" asked Mr Howard. His hair was aglow and the walls pulsed gently. Lisa put up her hand but then pulled it down slowly and shot it up in the air again. She did this a few times, mesmerised. Claire sat to Lisa's left, giggled and swooned.

"Lisa?" said Mr Howard.

"Mr Rochester," said Lisa, beaming. It was impossible to know whether she had forgotten Mr Howard's name or whether she was simply talking about the wrong book.

Claire was stroking her copy of Pride and Prejudice and crying. "There's no need for any of this," she said, her voice quiet and bleak.

"Sir," my voice came out too loud.

"Annie Marshall." He used my full name, and it made me feel important.

"I'm taking Claire out of class. She's not well." But then the bell went, and class was over anyway. I had no idea where those eighty minutes had gone.

Janey and I were free now, heading away from our classes and classmates. We were only a little bit trippy – I noticed my ears slipping gently and endlessly towards my neck while Janey was tapping her arm with her forefinger to see if it was solid. We started walking into town, down long empty Deane Road. The pavement smelled dusty in the sun, the terraced houses watched us, friendly. We waved at cars, who occasionally honked back at us, and we sang. "Say it's only a paper moon," at a passing Volvo Estate, "Hanging over a cardboard sea," at an XR2i. We'd been playing my parents' Ella Fitzgerald CD for weeks, all sophisticated.

We walked on the shady side of the road, and decided to twist our T-shirts at the front then tuck them over into the neckline, our sixteen-year-old midriffs in the open air and our 32A bras showing. A tee-kini! We got more honks after that but no lift which was fine because we were belting out our song, striding like jaguars and immune to other people.

Before we got as far as town there was Toys R Us, all solid and primary colours by the roundabout. A world of adventure. "We'll go and play," I told Janey. "We won't steal anything." Inside we found a corner with no apparent staff and mounds of plush, squidgy dogs and rabbits and cats. I plunged my arm into a pile of white puppies, right up to my elbow, and felt the softness and warmth. I compared my skin, the tiny criss-crosses and hairs, to the gleaming, lifeless fabric of the toys. "Everything that is good smells and moves," I told Janey, hugging her, smelling her.

We gave the little circling helicopters a wide berth on the way out, and ran the last five minutes into town. Sitting in the square, panting, I tried to work out where my lungs were. "Higher than you probably think," Janey informed me. "Way up here," she patted my shoulder, more or less. "Remember you've got to have room for your liver and your stomach too, they're all protected behind your ribs." I was besotted by the earnest teacherly tone in Janey's voice, but I knew better than to think for too long about my internal organs after taking acid.

We sat there on the steps in front of the town hall, in the full sun, watching Bolton. We tracked cute boys across the square, gazed all giddy when Neil Curtains and Hot Colin, sitting on a bench just outside Superdrug with their legs sprawling, took off their T-shirts, stretched their arms along the back of the seat and let their heads loll back, eyes closed to the light. Their necks were muscly, lumpy invitations, curving and pulsing. All warm.

"Should we eat soon?" Janey asked.

"I've got spliff at home." I had most of a bag left in my sock drawer, although my house was a bus ride away. "How can we get there?" The journey for a moment seemed unthinkable, and then we forgot that it was.

We walked part of the way, through the park making a list of the worst haircuts in history, and which character from EastEnders, if we really had to, we would shag.

"Roly!" I shouted, to make Janey laugh, and it did. When we saw the 617 coming we ran and caught it, the day still bright but now not warm enough for our silly bellies. We pulled our T-shirts back down, winked at a small grey-haired woman, felt rude, smiled.

"You'd know the world had been taken over by aliens," explained Janey, "if people got on the bus and filled up the seats in order, from the back corner, you know, one seat at a time."

Two girls who'd left our school the year before, dyed hair and Doc Martens, got on and gave us glancing smiles. Approval. They held on to the pole by the pram space, leaned back and swung gently.

My parents weren't home but we went straight up to my room anyway, stopping in the kitchen just to take a packet of chocolate digestives from the cupboard and to lift Clementine, our ginger cat, from the sofa.

"Who's got better coloured hair?" Janey asked, lying on my bed and tugging on her own copper hair, draping it over Clementine's head to give our cat a kind of toupee. Janey's hair used to change colour, quite dramatically and quite naturally – it was brighter in the summer and some kind of red forest universe in the winter.

"Can you still feel that trip?" I didn't mind that mine was gone, as long as Janey's had too.

"My arms feel kind of stretchy," she observed, extending an arm and contemplating its length, her fingers playing an invisible keyboard. "But maybe they just *are* a bit stretchy. It's time for some alcohol anyway."

So we got ready to go out with a bottle of Cointreau from downstairs sitting on my table next to the stereo and the moisturiser and the make-up. We took sticky sips and had quick showers and decided what to wear (Janey borrowed my white jeans again). It was a gentle excitement. We were in no hurry because the night was waiting for us, full of people and music and happy unknowns.

We got off the bus a stop early when we went back into town, so we could go to the corner shop and buy a flask each of Pernod – £4.49, fits into the back pocket of your jeans and tastes good poured into a pint of blackcurrant for 50p behind the bar at Fifth Avenue.

We never did have that spliff at my house, got distracted by the Cointreau, so we decided to take another half tab each before we went in. "Let's not get fucked," Janey said. "But let's get a bit fucked."

The entrance to Fifth Avenue had two bouncers, just inside the main door, and then you pushed through big silver doors into a dark room with low ceilings and lights, blue, red, green, yellow, jerking and swinging across the people.

What do I remember? That night, or maybe another night, I danced to Sylvester with a man I didn't fancy but who moved all fast and hips and fun. I kissed a man called James with long curly hair who was at least twenty-five. Which was old. Leanne was there with Unsy and Unsy's mate Clive, who talked a lot. Clive looked like a lizard, his eyes swung in their sockets and his skin was leather. While he talked, sitting down on the floor in the back of the room, the fire extinguisher behind him whispered over his shoulder, making it difficult to concentrate. The toilets were busy and we were desperate so we peed in the sinks. No one minded. Then later I went to the toilet again with Leanne's little brother who had cocaine. I thought he might kiss me but we just took the drugs. Christine and Rhona from Canon Slade didn't talk to me. They never liked me or Janey, I don't remember why.

Then "Let's go home," Janey said, and we did. It was a few years later that we got into the habit of staying to the very end of the night, or some way past it. On this night, we left early so we could miss the cheesy last song and get chips in pitta over the road without having to queue.

The taxi place was quiet too. It was still warm and two of the drivers sat outside, smoking and watching the drunk people. "Where you headed, girls?" His appearance didn't really register with me but the sight of his belly, just a pale hairy roll of it between his T-shirt and his jeans, lodged in my brain.

"Markland Hill," Janey told him. She was not entranced by the belly but was stroking the front of her face as if it was a cat. "Just by The French Arms."

"That whole street was bombed years ago, love, in the war." Not a glance to his mate, not a snigger, nothing. "We can't take you there."

Janey swung round, chin tucked down, and linked her arm into mine. She steered me away, taking short fast strides. "What's he talking about? Wanker. He knows we're fucked." Then she began to laugh and I did too. We were singing again.

"Summertime!"

We were yelling really, at the stars and the chimneys.

"And the living is e-e-e-easy!"

I started to cry when I remembered that this was the song my parents used to sing to me when I was very small. I felt lucky, I think, and guilty. I felt something, anyway, and I didn't want it to be nothing just because I'd had some drugs. Janey sat down next to me on the pavement.

"You're a good girl," she told me, stroking my shoulders, squeezing me. "We're good girls."

For a minute I thought the growling was Janey, trying to make me laugh. Then I growled back, and she said, "What are you growling at, dafthead?" Then, like slow-motion cartoons, we turned round to see an actual dog just behind us. Growling. He was behind a fence, which was good news because he was a dog that looked like a furry muscle with teeth. The fence was tall.

"Dogs know when you're tripping," said Janey, very quietly. This is true, I thought. The dog knows. He was in a frenzy of growling and twitching now. He was headbutting the fence. Janey had a look of delighted horror.

"Just walk slowly away," I told her. This was a serious situation requiring a serious voice. The dog stopped growling, watched us clinging together and shuffling down the pavement. Then we saw the gate, which was wide open.

"Ha!" Hysterical air shot from Janey's mouth. "Fence high," she said to me. Whispered. "Gate open."

"Fence high," I repeated. "Gate open." We swerved straight into the road, across to the other side, did not look back, and ran. The dog was probably inches from us, perhaps jumping at our backs. We kept on up the street and didn't turn round all the way home, although after a while we forgot about what we weren't looking back at.

My mum and dad had left the hall light on for us. I unlocked the back door, enjoying the fit of the key in the lock. Janey was thinking about the dog again.

"Fence high," she repeated. "Gate open. Fucking hell."

"Fence high," I said, putting my hands straight up in the air to demonstrate. "Gate open," I stretched my arms wide and pulled a silly face of panic.

"Shhhh!" Janey told me, giggling now, and we went in. Kettle and sofa and telly. Janey would sleep in the spare room, same as usual. I had a pair of pyjamas that I didn't wear anymore because I thought of them as Janey's pyjamas.

Janey sat on the kitchen floor in front of the open fridge while I made us Horlicks. She scooped houmous from a tub and into her mouth, using two fingers. In the next room, The Twilight Zone was just starting.

Then my dad appeared at the kitchen door in a T-shirt and boxer shorts. He blinked and shrank a little from the light. I was lost in the magic of how kettles know when to turn themselves off. Janey was humming to herself, although there was no tune as such.

"Did you two have a good night?"

"Yes, Mr Marshall!" sang Janey. She straightened her back and waved the tub of houmous as if it was proof of all the fun we'd had.

"Yes, it was fab," I said, teaspoon clinking on the mug.

"Good stuff. Sleep tight, then." And he stood for a couple of seconds in the doorway, his head tilted to one side, smiling.

At the Log Cabin by the Lake in the Middle of the Woods

They arrived in the afternoon, Karen and Claire, staring out each side of the taxi, gawping at the nature and the sky and the trees. It was a proper actual log cabin nestled at the edge of a woods by a lake. A loch. They tipped the driver a quid ("That's a lot of money in Scotland," Karen said) and stood on the gravel, looking out across the flat water to the mountains (bens, munros, whatever) on the other side, saying the things you're meant to say. "Wow!" and "Doesn't the air smell fresh?" and "The sky is so BIG here!" Claire stretched her arms wide, breathed in deep.

As promised by the weekend lettings company, the key to the cabin was on the ground by the front door under a stone carving – a hare, mossy in its crevices. When Karen pushed the big wooden door open, the creaking sound was so long and pitch-bending, so much like something from a BBC or Hammer Horror sound library, that she looked around as if she might see cameras or a man with a clapperboard.

Instead they saw two fat velvet sofas facing each other, perpendicular to a fireplace that was taller than them and wider than that, with a wood-burning stove inside, a box of logs beside it and still room for a seat – an inglenook. There was a low table between the sofas with piles of books – two old Agatha Christie paperbacks, and a little hardback guide to wild birds. Fitted dark-wood bookshelves filled the one wall, right up to the ceiling with a sliding ladder to get to the toppermost titles.

"This is not a log cabin, really, is it?" said Claire. She was laughing, slightly hysterical, nervous to go into the other rooms. She looked at the rows of books, imagined a hidden door which would open if you tugged on the right encyclopedia.

"It feels like someone's going to come and tell us that we can't really stay here," said Karen. "It's too nice."

This thought had half-occurred to Claire, too – that they were not the sort of people to stay in a place like this. Once Karen had said it out loud though she decided it was silly.

The bedroom had a bath in it, freestanding and with those claw feet, of course, in the middle of the room like a mythical metal pet. The bed was almost waist-height. Claire stood at the bedroom door and could see straight underneath it to the other side.

"Come on, we've left the bags outside," Karen said.

"Who's going to steal them?" Claire asked, still giddy and high-pitched. "A yeti?" She climbed onto the bed. It was big enough for Claire and Karen and a yeti, and a couple of spare yetis. From up there she felt like she might need to row, or steer, or order supplies in.

"The kitchen is full of food!" Karen screeched, and Claire sauntered through to have a look, giving it the laa-di-dah. There was an Aga, with a heavy pot full of carrots and potatoes and borlotti beans and tarragon and butter on top, keeping warm. A bowl of russet apples sat on the side next to a bottle of merlot, nice and warm-enough too, and a box of All Gold. Terry's All Gold! It was a small kitchen, compared to the cathedral-dimensioned sitting room, with two chairs at a wooden table, a jug with pink and purple anemones and a ridiculous silver candelabra.

"They said they'd leave some groceries and supper ready for us," said Karen, a lazy grin on her face as she adapted to this hifalutin life.

"Supper?"

"Tea, alright. Tea."

"I want to explore."

"There's a bathroom too."

"No, outside. Before it's dark."

They pulled the bags just inside the door and headed to the water, a few paces from the cabin. Claire looked down and the phrase 'crystal clear' stopped being a cliche, became a perfectly good description. Then she struggled for another.

"This water is like thick air," she said. "Thick, cold, soft air made for paddling in."

"Let's have a swim," said Karen.

She went to get towels from the cabin-castle and Claire stripped down to her knickers. Karen came back naked. "Not a soul around, not for miles," she grinned. "That's what the website said." She shook her belly and tits at the mountains.

The pebbles were cold and wet under their toes but the air was not cold, just fresh and soft, with no wind and a blanket of low sunlight covering them. Claire tugged her knickers to her ankles and stepped free of them. The full moon was already out – above the trees, yellowish and splodgy against the blue-white sky.

Karen ran straight in, making hurgh-hurgh noises, gasping and splashing, clumsy on the pebbles. Claire padded carefully down the rattling incline to the edge of the water.

"So cold!" Karen said, a loud bleat, with the water up to her chest. "My labia are retreating!" She was full of glee, fizzing with the chilly blast of it.

Claire stood there a bit longer. The trees came right down to the lake, along to her right, so many of them, tall and familial, a quiet gang watching. She stretched herself up, imagined as she lifted her arms that she might tickle the pale sky. Then she ran unsteady and eager into the water. She wanted to get in before

Karen got too cold and came out. She got knee-deep and then lay right back, held herself up with her hands, spun herself round and round, a rolypoly-ing water-baby.

"It's fine once you're in!" she said, which was sort-of true. Her skin was shrieking. Karen had swum out a few more metres and was floating on her back. "Look, Claire – the moon!" she shouted, and pointed to it, kicking her legs and wriggling to keep herself steady. Then she flipped over and swam a little more, a confident front crawl.

"It's colder the further out you come," Claire said, swimming towards Karen. She was wondering if she was out of her depth, aimed a pointed toe straight downwards like a ballerina and touched nothing.

They headed back up the pebbles and sat by the lake wrapped in the big towels. Claire fetched the wine and they swigged it. The cold of the water and then the clement air ("balmy," Karen said, "it's balmy!") had left their internal thermometers baffled, their skin neither hot nor cold but pink and alive.

Karen sighed.

"Do you miss Lucas?" Claire asked.

"Not right now I don't." Karen was holding the neck of the wine bottle, twizzling the concave base on her big toe. She looked like a child wrapped up out of the bath, playing, nearly ready for bed. "I miss Davey McLaverty from year five."

"From year five in school?" Claire thought she'd misunderstood.

"He was the nicest boy I ever went out with."

"In the fifth year?"

"He was fifth year, I was third year. I peaked early in love." She sighed again, and her bottom lip popped forward. "I finished with him because I wanted to get off with Si Twist. Si Twist said he wouldn't get off with me if I didn't finish with Davey first.

"Davey McLaverty wrote me poems and told me funny stories and brought me sweet presents," Karen was saying. "He was so kind. I thought they'd all be like that."

Karen and Claire had only really started hanging out together again in the last two months. Karen's boyfriend Lucas broke up with her on the same morning that Claire got turned down for a shitty promotion that she didn't even want and realised that she was going to leave her job. And so that lunchtime they both happened to be wandering, sulking, in the massive Topshop at Oxford Circus, looking at cheap bright gewgaws, like gamblers in a casino, about to be okay, any minute now. They'd recognised each other from college and compared petty miseries over neon lace vests. Then at lunchtime the next day they had a glass of wine in an actual winebar, and after that they made a habit, two or three days a week, of mooching around together at lunchtimes consoling one another.

Maybe if they weren't such recent friends, Claire would have said something when Karen started mooning over a school boyfriend from twenty years ago. She might have told her she sounded like a sappy character in a teen drama, not even Joey in Dawson's Creek, not even Tai in Clueless. Or she might have said, teasing, "Oh shit, can we rewind a couple of decades? Or shall we just go and pull an emotionally literate, sexually precocious fourteen year old, see how that works?" Instead she lifted the wine from Karen's limp hands and took a gulp. They sat and finished the bottle, it didn't take them long, looking out over the water snuggled in their towels.

Then they spent an hour trying to get the wood-burning stove to burn wood. They ate the stew with huge silver spoons, they drank another bottle of wine, they deliberated over the chocolates with tiptoeing fingers, like ladies in an advert. Cappuccino intrigue, vanilla flourish, midnight praline. They didn't mention that there wasn't a television in the cabin and they didn't turn the radio on. They opened a bottle of peaty whisky from the kitchen, slurped it from thick-bottomed tumblers, no ice and no water. Huge measures.

"Another one?" Karen would say.

"This stuff is beautiful," Claire would say, and offer up her glass. They took it in turns to pour, and the more they drank the more delicious it got.

Claire read the first few pages of The Secret Adversary, very slowly. Karen took the polish off her toenails. It was not quite nine o'clock. Claire went over to the bookshelves, looking for that hidden door.

From this groggy silence, they heard noises outside, something moving. Just in front of the cabin, perhaps. They looked each to the other, with did-you-hear-that-too eyes. There was no wind, so it wasn't the trees groaning or the water lapping on the pebbles. Then there was a great croaking howl, from the woods perhaps, and they both shrieked. They took a moment to feel silly, then they were just scared. A creak in the corner of the room and another more uncertain howl from the woods. Claire was on high alert, her ears trying to flap, to scan for sounds, her eyes wide, fingers splayed out straight like antennae switched on. Karen was on the floor by the stove, knees up, holding onto her toes, head thrown back, jaw frozen half open, blank and waiting. Claire was still at the shelves, no escape door to be found.

Then Karen grabbed the tongs, the massive pincers by the stove, and ran to the door, shoved her feet into her big boots. Claire started laughing, not a happy laugh. Tongs, she was thinking, not even a poker, as if there might be a barbecue out there in the dark rather than a wild animal or an axe murderer. She thought of how Karen played in their after-work football games at Regent's Park, steaming towards the goal, shouting "Attack! Attack!", laughing like a maniac, roaring at the opposition.

She was outside now, had left the door agape. Claire looked at the almost-empty whisky bottle and it occurred to her that she could close the door, lock it, stay inside by the stove with the chocolates and that paperback. Still, here she was, grabbing her coat, pulling on her boots, heading out after Karen.

A vertigo took hold of Claire when she stepped outside, her sense of scale toppled over. Their grand posh cabin became a stupid box and this was stars and moon and space, the surface of the lake a not-there barrier to another world beneath, the trees all various but all the same and pulling you in for adventures.

She saw Karen disappear into the woods, hunting, and headed after her, propelled by admiration and a desire to witness the main event. But her stride slowed to a syrupy stumble once she reached the trees, and each step became a new discovery – a log, was that?, a stone, something spongy, something cracking under her boot. There was a sound just behind that may have been her own footsteps, or may have been something else. She noticed that she didn't care about Karen anymore or what the howling had come from. She wasn't worried now, she just felt cosseted. The woods held her. The trees were so straight, so straight up, that the moon created pale blue stripes and long triangles. The dim, oozing light made everything seem flat so she couldn't entirely tell if a tree, a rock, a branch was inches or yards away. The woods smelled clean, alive. She would like to have spent months, years, decades exploring the rough scabby bark on those trees, the mosses firm and soft like a just-baked cake, the pine needles under her feet, countless tiny spines, soft in their millions, the beetles pacing their territories, the spiders spawning spiders.

She fell over, ker-bomp, and zoomed her face right in next to a root that was knuckling out of the ground, slipped her hand around and took hold of it like you would a doorhandle. Her eyes struggled to focus, up so close to the bark ravines and the gristly lumps. It smelled good. Things were alive in there and busy. Her smile pulled up the corners of the earth like a rug. *A darkness has consumed my soul*, she remembered, and that felt good.

There was another howl, but she noticed it some while after it had happened, as if she'd been asleep and was trying to recall the noise that woke her up. She looked straight up to the moon then closed her eyes to enjoy the soft round memory it left on her lids. She lay back and waited with her eyes wide to see what might pour in. But nothing else appeared and there were no more howls. She relaxed back into the ground, closed her eyes, felt safe. Limply, she wondered where Karen might have got to, how long they'd been outside. Was it getting cold? Damp?

So she pushed and pulled herself up and took a few steps, into a treeless patch of ground and then just beyond that, where she saw something hanging in the trees. It was a branch, snapped off and dangling there, except actually it looked like Karen. It was the right size, that cluster of leaves could be her hair and profile, lit by the moon, that smaller branch her floppy feet. She stared at it, trying to see a branch instead of a dead friend. She held down a tickling panic, felt her brain teetering.

And Claire was tired so she sat back on the soft ground. Something was rising, singing inside her. Then there was heavy breath a few yards to the right and then there was Karen, real alive Karen, leaning up against a tree, rolling herself around it. She had dropped the tongs at her feet, and she sank her face and chest into the tree's bark, one cheek pushed up like a pillow for her eye. Her face was puffy and streaked with snot and tears for Davey McLaverty or Lucas or whatever, but she was not crying now. She was on pause, held there by the tree, not asleep or awake, like a big stupid baby. I could pick up one of these hefty branches, thought Claire, and I could walk over and smash her fucking head right in.

And then Claire noticed the stag. How ridiculous. A stag tottered right into the clearing and stopped in the moonlight. He stopped and looked at Claire. He was too far away to touch but near enough that she could see his pulsing neck. His breath was fast and quiet, he was square and still, bones and skinny legs, improbable antlers and a round solid softness. She watched, listened, kept quiet, tried to breathe shallow and silent. The stag blinked, slowly, and his head shifted a little. He was real. Claire didn't move, felt her skin like stone. The stag kept her still, and it felt calm, exciting.

And then he went, haughty and magnificent, breezy and powerful, away into the woods. Gone. Usual life came slumping back in, all blah-blah-blah. For a while Claire watched the space where the stag had been, the trees still glowing with the memory of him.

Karen whimpered. Her eyes were closed, she hadn't seen the stag. Claire was up and walking over to her, grabbed her, loving and rough like a matinee idol. Karen grinned, was happy to be found. She gave a snorting little giggle, like a drunken, too-old starlet who thinks she's still cute.

"Let's get back to the cabin," Claire said, one arm around her friend now. "I'll put the kettle on, get you safe to bed."

When Can You Start?

I was going to a job interview, I was supposed to be getting a new job, but I knew if I concentrated hard enough I'd make it here, to a sunny dusty avenue in the Pyrenees with a cold glass of wine and tiny French birds chirruping in the trees. *Les moineaux.* They are singing. *Ils chantent.*

I'm wearing a fitted skirt, just below the knee, and I'm wearing heels but the heels are lace-ups so they feel secure on my feet. And a long-sleeved T-shirt, but quite a posh one (linen blend), tucked in, with what my mum might have called a 'snazzy' belt.

The interview – the job – is at Vogue House. Condé Nast, posh magazines. This place has class, I say to myself as I walk in: class, pizazz and gravitas. They should use that as a slogan, except they're too classy and gravitassy to do that. It's on Berkeley Square, on the corner. You push through the revolving doors and the air conditioning begins to suck the hot dampness from you. The foyer is marble and glass, high ceilings. The floor is a bit slippy but my heels have rubbery tips so I am fine, thanks. I'm very nearly strutting. Piece of string from the crown of my head. There's flowers and seats and magazines.

I am friendly to the receptionist, a young man who looks like he's doing summer-holiday work experience. I'm friendly and professional, bright and serious. There's no one here but us two. I announce myself and wonder how many other people they're interviewing today. There's no signing-in book, nowhere to have a quick peek and see who else has been here. The boy picks up a phone, seems to know what he's doing, speaks to someone upstairs, looks back to me.

"Fifth floor, please, Ms Marshall," he grins. "Debra will meet you outside the lift."

Who's Debra? He doesn't say. Maybe I'm supposed to know.

"Thanks so much," I say. Thanks so much? How much?

Everything, everything, everything, everything

The lift arrives and it's full-length mirrors in there so I get a chance to look at my professional, creative self. Check my make-up is intact. No food stuck in the teeth. A bit of sand is still clinging to the bottom of my legs, just a few grains, soft and salty round my ankles. It's rather attractive, kind of sexy. I look capable, I look stylish, you'd trust me to edit your celebrity interviews, check your page furniture, you could invite me down the pub, maybe share some sushi at lunchtimes. I stand and face the doors, all set for that fifth floor. I'm glad there's no one else in the lift. I try to relax my face, get my expression Debra-ready.

It's so hot today, I wish my tits were smaller so I didn't have to wear a bra. Who wants nylon and wire clamped onto you in this weather? Nobody. Little tits and I could let the breeze to my nipples, but with these I need a bit of lift and containment, else they get in the way. Even on holiday.

"Hi, Annie!"

Debra seems nice.

"Thanks for coming in. We're just down here on the left."

She leads me past banks of desks, bookshelves filled with cardboard boxes and piles of folders. Big windows and a few pot plants, a warm breeze and sea air. Glass partitions. Then she opens a door and nods me inside. I recognise Elise, the editor, from her photo in the front of the magazine. She's sitting there with another woman who's looking at an A4 sheet on the table in front of her, crossing things off a list. Or maybe doing a wordsearch, or a sudoku, like you do on holiday.

Everything, everything, everything, everything

"Hi, Annie!" says Elise. Everyone is really delighted that I'm here. "Take a seat. This is Maddy."

Maddy looks up and smiles too. "I'm the associate editor," she tells me. Pretty fancy.

Debra's still at the door. "Would you like anything to drink?" she asks. "Tea? Coffee?"

"I'd love a gin and tonic."

"Ice and lemon?"

"Lovely, yes. Well, actually lime if you have it, otherwise lemon is fine." I think lime is a bit more exciting. Just a little bit, obviously I'm not actually excited by lime.

"I'll see what we have," says Debra. She doesn't look hopeful about the limes.

I'm invisible, I'm invisible, I'm invisible, I'm invisible

"We're really impressed with your CV," Elise tells me. She's wearing the same sort of outfit as me, except more expensive. Her belt isn't snazzy though. "Can you tell us a bit about why you've applied for this role?"

Maddy's pen is poised.

Everything, everything, everything, everything

"Well, I really enjoy the work I'm doing at the moment," I say. "I love the office too, it's a good little company and I've learned a lot."

Elise is nodding, Maddy is waiting to write something.

"What I want now is to dig in deeper. I want to write more, I want to travel more, I want to meet more people and try new things."

Elise is nodding and smiling now. Maddy still hasn't written anything.

"And the work you do here, the character of this magazine – that's something I'd like to be involved with. Style, fresh ideas, a real interrogation of new fashions and trends, you know?"

Now Maddy is making some notes, or doodling.

"I mean, if you're going to work on something for eight or nine hours a day, five or six days a week, you have to care about it, don't you?"

A rueful smile from Elise. Rueful and fond. I think she likes me.

"Is it a croque madame that's vegetarian?" I ask. I can't remember. It's tricky being vegetarian in France. People keep trying to give you tuna and anchovies. I'm not peckish or anything, I'm just wondering. I had some oeufs mayonnaise for my lunch, with a glass of very cold, very pale rosé. The bouncy curves on the eggs were wonderful, the slippery mayonnaise and the boing and the flavour.

"Absolutely," says Elise. "Can you tell us a bit more about your current role, the responsibilities you have there?"

I stretch in my chair a bit, adjust my posture, engage those core muscles. Debra pops in with my gin and tonic and I give her a smile and a wink.

Why don't you call me, I feel like flying.
Why don't you call me, I feel like flying

"I oversee the production, keep everything running smoothly and keep the schedule front-loaded as much as possible," I say. "Lots of nudging and encouraging. I try to run a tight but friendly ship!"

Elise smiles, perhaps imagining a tight and friendly ship.

"And recently I'm doing much the same with the online content. There are different challenges there, but I think it's vital that we give it the same, like, forensic attention."

Maddy is writing, and nodding.

"I work with the editor on plans and ideas for the future, too – the month-to-month nitty-gritty and the longer term identity of the magazine, where we're headed over the next couple of years and more."

Everything, everything, everything, everything

I put my shoulders back, feel the leather of the chair against my back and slippery under my skirt. My hand is rubbing the back of my neck. I look at Elise, smile at her. Then I realise my head's tilted back as if I'm about to eat her, so I tuck my chin down a bit and try to look meek but also steely.

"And do you get to do much writing at the moment?"

"Oh, lots of short news pieces and occasionally an interview or a longer feature. I'd like to do more, that's one of the reasons I'm looking to move."

"Well, you'd certainly get plenty of opportunity to write here. We like the pieces you sent over very much."

"And it'd be great to have you managing some of our younger writers," says Maddy.

"Oh, I'd like that," I say. I give a motherly smile, nurturing, inspiring even.

"We could introduce you to Frank, head of editorial devel-opment," she says. "He's our talentspotter, always looking for more people to help with his schemes for getting new young writers in."

I picture this unknown Frank as an actual talentspotter, like a benevolent childcatcher, in a special costume perhaps, looking for young people with ripe ideas. I feel a tiny wave of sadness that I am no longer quite a young person with ripe ideas.

I'm invisible, I'm invisible

"This job is just maternity cover, though, as you know," says Maddy.

"Yes," I say. "That's fine with me, I can probably only stay for a couple of weeks."

"We can guarantee it for a year, although it may go on a bit longer. It really depends on Victoria and when she decides to come back."

"No problem," I say. "Totally fine."

Everything, everything, everything, everything

Three small-ish children are playing by the fountain, about ten yards away on the dusty avenue. Their parents are in another cafe, across the road from me and just past the fountain. Two men, my age, and two women, who are looking happy and relaxed, talking, smoking. I can't quite hear them and I can't tell who's with who, or which children belong to which adults. They all have tanned white skin and very dark hair. Maybe they're all related, one big extended family, siblings and cousins on holiday together. Maybe I'm in the quiet, nice sort of place where chi-chi French people go on holiday. I watch the children at the fountain. Two small girls dipping their hands right into the water, and one even smaller boy with a little truck or a car, zoom-zooming it around the stone edge of the fountain. Kids are great, but I don't think I want to have any.

"Kids are great," I say. "But I don't think I want to have any."

"They're little terrors," laughs Maddy. "I love mine, but they are little terrors."

Elise doesn't say anything about children. I don't know if she has any. She's very slim, but she looks quite tired.

"Little terrors," I say. "Ha!"

I take another suck of my icy gin and tonic, in its tall glass with a long straw. Just a few feet away from me sits a sturdy leathery old man in a soft navy cap, his little dog beside him, slurping a cold pastis on his way home. I like to see old locals on holiday. Authentic, grumpy, cool, something like that. He's actually got the baguette he just bought on the table, wrapped in a bit of greaseproof paper. I bet he'll eat it with salty butter and some good jam. Or gooey cheese. I mean, fucking hell, eh? Life's about priorities.

"Ooh, you were at special projects at Natmags for a while – did you work with Sallie there?" Elise is just perusing my CV now, making conversation. I imagine they've already decided whether or not I'll get the job.

"Oh yes, we were on production together. That was one of my first magazine roles. She was great to work with."

"She's certainly indispensable here."

Elise is smiling and Maddy is writing something again. I wonder what Sallie will say when they ask about me. We always got on. We used to play darts at the pub together at lunchtimes. Once I went with her to the walk-in clinic when she had a strange, sudden rash up her thigh. I'm not sure she ever found out what it was.

Right across from me there's a broad doorway, wooden, with cast iron hinges and a cast iron handle. It has a stone stoop and on that stoop there's a ginger cat, stretched out on its back. His tail is in the shade but he's mostly in the sunshine, his white and ginger furry belly up in the air, ready for a tickle. Except you know most cats actually don't like it when you stroke them on their belly. It's a bit much. Another cat, a black cat and much smaller, is a couple of feet away. They must know each other, these cats. The black cat is almost still a kitten, and skinny. Wants feeding. I hope they'll come over, say hello, rub against my leg, give me a nose bump. I don't suppose they like pastry, or coffee, but I can offer them strokes and scruffles behind the ear.

I'm invisible, I'm invisible, I'm invisible, I'm invisible

"We're interviewing a few more candidates, today and tomorrow," Elise tells me. "And then we'll be in touch as soon as we can."

"Great," I say. "Great."

Why don't you call me, I feel like flying in two.
Why don't you call me, I feel like flying in two

"You should hear from us before the end of the week, with any luck."

"Great," I say. I'm pleased that's all over, and that it went so well. I think it went well. I lean right back, take a slow deep breath, relaxing in the sunshine. The ice has almost melted in my drink, pink and blue light is somehow caught in the glass. The birds are darting between the trees, they've got their own thing going on. I feel the clamminess in my armpits and between my legs. I wiggle my toes in the heat. I am fleshy and warm and ever so happy.

"Good to meet you," Elise says, rising from her seat. Maddy doesn't get up, but she gives me a lovely big smile. The sun is shining through the office window onto her pale blonde hair. You can see that her shoulders would burn in five minutes in this weather. I bet she uses factor 50.

Everything, everything, everything, everything

"The pleasure's all mine," I say, and decide I'll order another drink. The sun will soon begin to soften into evening, the colours in the wide avenue will get richer, the shadows will get longer. I'll have maybe one more drink after this one, watch the people walk by, watch those sparrows – *les moineaux*, my lips purse twice with the word – in the trees, and think about where I might have dinner tonight.

A Shania Story

"Hey Annie!" Stella looks at me, one eyebrow raised. "What would you say is the best thing about being a woman?"

"Oh," I say. "Surely it's the prerogative to have a little fun? You know, go totally crazy."

"Forget you're a lady?"

No one else in the queue finds this funny. They are not Shania Twain fans, and they do not appreciate juvenile in-jokes based on Shania Twain lyrics.

Stella and I are savvy, sexy, sassy, that kind of thing. We are drunk. We are waiting to get into Frankie's Bar. This is a cool place to be. A cool band is playing later, and although we are not on the guest list we feel pretty cool. We are breezy and powerful. We've been trying to shake off the two men with us since we left the pub. Stella knows them from work, and they are blocking our dazzle. They stand too close and they have aggression just under their skin, just under their nice-blokeness. Their mums, me and Stella would agree, were too soft with them. Any girl would be lucky to have them, apparently, they're a catch. Imagine.

Once we're inside, the dark and the noise and the lights and the faces fill us up, sweep us away. The DJ plays a song which is not I Feel Love but which sounds enough like I Feel Love to make me and Stella smile and swoon and spin round and round. Hundreds of people are smiling and swooning and spinning around, smiling at each other in the dark with the blue and red lights, and nothing more is asked of us.

Then Stella and I slip sideways, away from the two cock-blockers, zigzagging through the bodies and into the smaller room off to one side, the room where you have to know some-one to get in. Janine on the door knows me, likes me, and we're through. Warm, swaying people rub past each other. My eyes are wide. Craig Darling who works at Dazed is at the back by the bar next to Oli from High-A Records. The cute but gak-fatty A&R who is at every gig I go to is talking to a woman I met at Grace's 40th birthday when we mixed MDMA into the punch and cried when Lou played Everywhere by Fleetwood Mac. None of us says hello.

I love the faces and the clothes and the haircuts and the shoes, the way people lean in to each other to talk, throw back their heads to laugh, tilt their heads to listen. I love how the music covers the conversation, thuds into our ribs, pulls us all together like bass stock for people soup. I love the possibilities and the dancing, and the being alone, together, in the dark, late in the night. I love the faces that I've only ever seen at night, people I know more about than they've ever told me.

There's a carpet in this room and amber uplights behind the bar, making the bottles of whiskey and vodka and gin glow. So classy. When I see the bass guitarist from the band heading over I lean back, look over my shoulder, try to aim my profile in his direction, do a slow blink. He curves through and lands in the spot next to me.

"What time are you on?" I grin, I'm happy. He remembers me from a gig last week and hugs me. Turns out they've played already. He smells of warm skin and sweat and cigarettes. I think he smells American but it's because his American accent is leaking into all my senses. His voice is slow and carefree. It makes things feel less real. He tells me I'm super-fucking-rad, which is of course ridiculous but also I love it. Stella has gone for another dance.

So I talk to the bass player and the rest of the room is turned down. I am absorbed by him and by what he might be thinking about me. It is giddy and simple.

"We're having a party at the hotel," he says, which is an invitation in not-bothered disguise.

His bandmate, the drummer, tells me, "It will ruin our trip if you don't come back to the party with us. My heart will break."

The drummer is short and wiry, he looks like he's about to bounce away, like you should be bouncing away with him. He passes me a bottle of Jack Daniel's which is not, obviously, allowed in a carpeted bar with amber uplights. I take a swig and I enjoy the cheesiness, the bullshit. I am a cowboy, all muscle and swagger. The whiskey doesn't burn at all. The bass player is talking to another man, hairy and muscly, a roadie or a sound guy, about where their van is. The bar is busy with noise and people but Stella is back again and bored of the music and we are ready to leave. We have completed this level.

The drummer licks my shoe and tells us where the band's hotel is. There are other people heading there too but Stella and I go to get a taxi on our own because we are in no mood for logistics. We are headlong, we are night people, towering.

Outside the club, the street is wet and dark. We look for yellow lights.

"Ooh it's like an Edward Hopper painting," I say, in a silly, airy voice.

"I need a wee," says Stella, scanning around for a welcoming, private spot. She reels imperious across the street and through revolving doors into a hotel lobby. Quite a posh hotel, middle of town, dark wood and green coloured glass. I follow her. Nothing can go wrong because we are drunk and the world is ours. And it's only a hotel lobby. With toilets – we have a wee then sit on the comfy chairs by the basins.

"So nice that you can just walk in here," I say. I snuggle down a bit in the seat. "And they have handcream. I love that. The world is so good."

Stella takes off her pumps and washes her feet in the sink.

"Hang on," I say. "Is that allowed?"

"I want that handcream on my toes," she says. She rubs it in and all in between. Then she does mine, although I do not wash my feet first. Then I pick the black shit out of the corner of my eyes, and we are back outdoors.

Across the street, the bass player and the drummer and the hairy man are right there at the door of the club, their van fully loaded. There's room for me and Stella though, and we climb in.

"It's like Scooby-Doo," Stella says. The drummer woofs. We are hilarious. London's daytime cafes and shops are wet and empty, dark. No people. We are snug in the van, peering out of the windows, with R Kelly on the stereo. We wait at traffic lights, sing along in silly voices, "Sipping on coke and ru-uum, I'm like, So what, I'm dru-uunk."

I am not sitting next to the bass player. He looks at me, over and over, and I try to sit up straight but kind of slouchy too, like I haven't noticed.

Their hotel is huge, Victorian, white and pillars, up a wide avenue. It has a lobby with too many patterns, and more comfy chairs, sofas, tables with ashtrays and glasses full of ice and booze. One man is asleep, lying across a sofa, and another man gently lifts the first man's legs so he can sit there. He puts the legs back down, across him, like the safety bar on a fairground ride.

Two men and two women are sitting round a little table, leaning forward, elbows on knees. I saw them at Frankie's, with their heavy fringes and wide eyes. Their voices clatter and overlap, they are panicked with things to say – ooh yes me too, yes, I know that one, I've been there, oh you would love it, it was amazing, yeah. There is no music playing but the band's singer is humming a tune and giggling, talking to a woman who is dangling a bottle of Southern Comfort in front of him like a pendulum while a man is tickling him in the ribs.

I spot a piano in the corner and I run over, all excited. Stella and I sit on the keys and bounce up and down along the piano. "Bum chopsticks!" Stella shouts, and the drummer starts to bang on the piano stool. We are idiots. The bass player has another bottle of Jack Daniel's on the floor next to him and half a bottle of Southern Comfort in his hand. Now Stella is talking to the pendulum woman and the tickling man. The drummer is playing piano, concentrating like a little boy at a lesson. He plays the theme from The Exorcist and sings, "I wanna go to Mars." I sit and sway and fade a little, and feel the quiet softness of things. I sit like this for a while. He sings and plays. The Jack Daniel's is good but the Southern Comfort is better.

I go to explore – to find the toilets – and see the morning seeping through the front door of the hotel. I like it, a soft pearl light heading our way. And, as I thought, as I knew, when I come out of the bathrooms and cross the hallway to get back to the party, there's my bass player. He's walking up the stairs, which are shallow and wide and swoop around and up. He's walking slowly and when he sees me he smiles and sits down, near the top of the stairs. He's wearing what Stella and I refer to as lee-zure slacks, and a white vest with a short-sleeved shirt over the top. He is chubby and cute, greasy brown hair and blue eyes. He looks like an American boy who plays bass and tours in a cheap van with a half-decent band. I walk up the stairs and I don't care about him or what he's like. I care about his sticky, late-night skin and his boozy, flabby belly. He's revolting and appealing.

"I've got more whiskey in my room," he tells me. Which is another invitation. His room has more patterns and twin beds, and a window looking over the backs of big expensive houses. He sits on the bed and tucks his fingers into my waistband, pulls me away from the view.

"C'mere" he says. I fall onto the soft bed. Lying down is a good idea I should have had hours ago. The bass player pulls my jeans right off, without undoing the buttons. I notice this like you'd notice a car door slamming outside. I suppose he pulls my pants off too. I feel a knocking in my brain, you have to do something now, time to do something.

You are supposed to have sex now, once you're in the room with your knickers off. He is clammy and on top of me, trying to fold his not-quite-hard penis into me. I kiss him, which is to balm the embarrassment or to make him feel he is not a vile, lurching thug of a failure. I don't feel a thing when he's pushing into me, huffing into my ear, except his weight on my chest. I pull my knees right up but it makes no difference. Drink has deadened me from the waist down. I'm going to stop pretending now so I pull away, slide to one side. He pulls me over and on top of him, so I keep going. From here I can pull on his sticky skin, push and twist his doughy stomach. I push the heel of my hand into his ribs and wonder what's in there. Which is not his idea of fun so he rolls over on top of me again. I tell him no and I push him off me. "What, you came already?" he asks, a bit annoyed. I head to the bathroom and sit on the toilet. It's quiet and warm and peaceful in there, solid walls around me. When I go back to bed and lie down he rolls on top of me again without saying a word.

"Is this, is wha-," I say.

"Shhh," he says, all gently in my ear. I move around and make noises to try to hurry it up. Then I say, "Come on my belly, baby, come on my belly," because I think he probably isn't wearing a condom. Maybe my accent sounds sexy to him.

"You want me to come on you," he says, not a question, all husky and delighted. I guess he does because when I wake up, he has.

The drummer is there, asleep on the next bed, in his Eyehategod T-shirt and his dirty skinny jeans and Converse. The door opens and another man walks in with two paper cups of coffee. I have never seen him before. I pull my pants and jeans on, slowly and without turning away.

The coffee man says hello, shakes my hand. He's American too, thinks it's English and proper and funny to shake my hand.

"You want this, honey?" he asks. He gives me the drummer's coffee and puts the other one down very slowly and carefully on the little table between the beds.

"I'll take it with me." I want to be outside on my own under the autumn sky with a hot drink in my hand. The bass player, who is now rubbing my lower back, pulls on his lee-zure slacks and walks me out to the hallway.

"Nice to meet you," and he slides one hand down my breast and belly. "No babies, okay?" He's swaying a little. It is too late to make things nice but I try when I smile at him and say, "You too," and try to look wholesome and like I'm in his gang. The corridor is dimly lit and I'm not sure which direction to go in so I stride down and wait until I hear their door close. Then I just keep striding, to find out if I'm going the right way. The stairs are shallow and wide and they swoop around and down.

The day has been here for hours, so I'm out of sync when I walk out of the big front door and turn left onto the pavement and straight ahead and then left again and wonder where I am.

There's the park across the road. Here's a street sign with a postcode I'm not usually in.

I call Stella and she's at work, in the office but taking naps in the toilets, she tells me, every hour or so, "like a tramp with a computer and a salary". She's eaten a veggie burger from the cafe over the road, a chunky Kitkat, four mugs of tea, a bottle of Purdey's and three glasses of water with two Berocca in each of them.

Her voice is giddy. She got a taxi home at five. She doesn't ask me about the hotel and I don't tell her anything, just what the street signs say so she can look it up online and tell me which direction to walk in.

Then she hangs up, off to buy more Purdey's, and I think about the speed of the traffic rushing past me on Bayswater Road, the weight of each vehicle. Mass times acceleration equals feel better now. I look at the kerb and I think about the here and the there. Here and over there, not far at all. The leaves on the trees are turning, and falling.

Pussycat

Consent is clear with my pussycat. Her soft white belly all furry fluff with those little pink nipples that I can't quite see. Six of them, is it, or eight? I can't go near that belly, she'd bite me or – slightly more likely – she'd bite me and then she'd dig every one of her claws – four paws and I don't know how many claws – into the tender base of my thumb, the back of my hand, my wrist, my forearm. Blood and pain and clarity. Consent is clear with my pussycat.

Lauren, Our Path Emerges For a While

Where is Lauren? Is she in the muddy rotting leaves under our feet? Is she in my muscle and bone, did I eat her, reabsorb her, burn her up like fuel? She is underneath the surface of the water, apparently, ready to talk, laugh, listen, hug me, curl up on my lap like she did when she was a baby, my little girl with her small shoes and brown eyes and her sweet fat cheeks.

Lauren is dead and I miss her. Lauren is dead dead dead and I miss her.

A few weeks ago I was out on the heath for the first time in a long time, and I saw Lauren's best friend, Claire, her best friend from school and her best friend right up until Lauren was killed in that car. It's been decades, but I recognised Claire, even from a distance, without a moment's pause, and she recognised me. I saw her demeanour change: she recoiled very slightly as if a cold gust had hit her in the face, and then she leaned forward and her pace became more deliberate. She walked towards me on the path, with all the years on her that Lauren doesn't have. She stopped and we hugged and I think we conjured Lauren with our coincidence. I'd say I hugged her for too long but she also hugged me for too long, so we were in agreement there. We said hello and how are you, and she wasn't in a hurry, she said, so she walked with me for a while and this is what she told me.

"Me and Lauren lay just over there one summer, warm on the grass, and she recited a poem. We'd done it for A-level and she knew it by heart. You'll know it, too, it's really famous – the one with the days of wine and roses."

Claire stopped and looked the whole poem up on her smartphone and read part of it out loud, there on the path, reading the same lines to me that my daughter had read to her that afternoon on the grass:

> "They are not long, the days of wine and roses:
> Out of a misty dream
> Our path emerges for a while, then closes
> Within a dream.

"We swam in the pond that day," she went on. "It was baking hot by late afternoon, and then as it got dark we went to The Wells Tavern.

"I can't go to that pub anymore, I haven't been in there since, but I go to the pond a lot. She's there with me, she's there in the water. Sometimes, I dive in and I pretend that I'm out at Valentino's in town again with Lauren and we are alive and safe and dancing among the columns of light in the darkness and our bodies moving with more sense and more magic now that we're under the water and on the dancefloor. We loved dancing so much, Mrs Fletcher, we loved the glamour of it and the seediness, although we wouldn't have described it like that at the time. It felt like we were practising for an exciting and glamorous grown-up life that never came, for either of us. And now I go under the water in the swimming pond and I picture the evidence left on the surface as I go beneath, and I know that Lauren is in those tiny winking bubbles and that she's with me down there.

"There's a lot I've forgotten, most of it maybe. I wish I could remember just one conversation, word for word, one full conversation with Lauren. We must have had conversations, right, I'm not going mad? People have conversations. But I do remember walks, and dancing, and poems, and songs. I remember singing 'Oo-ooh child, things are gonna get easier,' after we heard it in a film, and I sing it to myself sometimes now, even though I know it's not true.

"You know, Mrs Fletcher, I felt for years that I had left her behind, that I had rudely carried on without her, living my life, seeing the world, or a bit of it, and meeting new friends, falling in love, having kids, building a career. And now, as I get older and I get tired and I get disappointed, by all of it, you know, disappointed by me and by everywhere I go and everything I do and everything I see, now I feel that she was the one who went on ahead without me."

"I feel like that too," I told Claire. "I feel like that too."

"Lauren got to skip all this," Claire went on. "She missed the disappointments as well as the joys.

"But I do find joy in the feeling of my warm toes wiggling in my woolly socks in my clomping boots or in the feeling of a deep breath in cold air, and when I feel good I imagine Lauren feeling good too.

"I don't want to sound too mad, Mrs Fletcher, but even though I know she is dead and even though I was at the funeral and before that I visited her at the funeral home and after that I stood with you as they put her into the ground and we threw the flowers on top, and I remember that but I also feel the ongoing possibility that Lauren is not dead. She is here and I am a puppet for her, a loving proxy, I give her the feeling of sunshine on my cheek and a giddy giggle when a cute guy smiles at me in the street, but I don't give her the creaking hips or the layers of tiredness or the slow feeling of horror, real horror, as I watch my husband become this floppy dullard, and my own small enthusiasms in life seem to repel him, and I'm right there with him, cringing at myself, really, just stuck here. Just stuck here."

Claire didn't tell me much about her life or her job or her husband or her kids. Maybe I should have asked more. I mentioned that I was divorced now from Lauren's dad but she already knew that.

"He was a good man," I said. "But the loss was too much for us. The grief was too much to share."

"You were both so kind to me," Claire said. "I remember coming round to your house a couple of days after the funeral and you fed me dinner. I didn't have the sense to fully realise that I wasn't having the worst time of it, out of all of us." She was crying now, there on the heath. "I'm sorry."

"Don't you be sorry," I told her. "We loved having you come round. We missed you when you moved away."

"Your house felt so safe," she told me, remembering. "Lauren's dad at the stove, clattering and humming. The kitchen was steamy, it smelled warm and homey. I remember going upstairs and lying on Lauren's bed for a bit. I could hear you and Mr Fletcher talking, the sounds came up through the floorboards, and pan lids and cutlery. When you shouted 'Dinner's ready!' and I pretended I was Lauren, and I kept very still, there on her bed for a few seconds longer. Then when I got to the bottom of the stairs I stopped again, put my hands on that big wooden sideboard you had, flat on the top with my fingers stretched out like it was a ouija board. You must have heard me come down and I could hear you in the next room, not talking, a tap of a spoon on a bowl, maybe, a knife on a plate. I remember this so clearly, Mrs Fletcher, but why don't I remember more about Lauren?

"You were already looking up at the doorway when I walked in, with a soft smile on your face. Lauren's dad looked like he was going to cry, shoulders sagged, chin slack, looking at his plate. Everything was so slow and heavy.

"And then Lauren's dad began talking about using parsley instead of coriander or something, and you said about doing the weekly shop at Sainsbury's in the morning, and Mr Fletcher was almost cheery, talking about the garden. I didn't say a word, I had nothing to say. The radio was on, you two were talking, and I just sat there like a lump. And you never looked at one another in that silent coded way, never excluded me in that sharp fast moment of exchanged glances. I was so grateful for that. Kind people, you were, Mrs Fletcher, full of kindness. You have to be so vigilant, to be kind."

And then, and then, and then. Me and Mrs Fletcher met up again a week later, by the pond. On purpose, this time, early one evening when the pond was officially closed – you can always sneak in and I frequently do. Lauren's mum walked ahead on the path, too keen almost to get to the pond. I could not quite keep up and wondered if I'd offended, somehow. Offended would not be the right word though: I was driving that car and Lauren was dead and I had, as they say, not a scratch on me.

Lauren was taller and leaner than me. She was a few months older too, February to my July. And so we walked together, more or less the same but not quite.

"It's pretty here," I said, thinking of the birds and maybe squirrels. If we'd stopped and kept still for a minute we might have heard some birdsong, or some rustling in the trees and bushes. We got to the gate and it wasn't closed properly, never mind locked. The changing rooms were empty and so was the lifeguards' hut. The wooden platform extended over the water, and a ladder ran down into the black.

I say black, actually the pond reflected light from the sky, which was now a properly dark-blue night sky, clear and starry.

The moon was somewhere, not in sight but giving a flattening light. There were ripples on the water, and a couple of little ducks. I loved those ducks.

"I brought us bath towels," she said, smiling and lifting her shoulders round her ears, as if she was damp and cold and someone had just wrapped a great big fresh bath towel right around her. We had a flask of tea, too, with lots of sugar in it.

She folded her glasses and placed them on top of her bag, put goggles over her wide-open eyes. She'd already peeled down to her swimming costume, which she'd had on under her clothes. She gave a "brrrr!" of delight, but that was before she was in. When she sank into the pond she was quiet, and so was the water.

I changed into my red bikini with the elastic threads sticking out all over it like tiny worms, I'd had it for years. My clothes were on a bench and I was on the ladder, holding on behind me and facing out into the water, having a look, like a carved woman on the front of a ship. Mrs Fletcher was halfway across the pond already.

"Come on in," she said, in a shout-whisper because we were illicit there. "Come on in, the water's lovely!" I was meant to be showing her around because she'd never been here before, but she didn't need me. She glided over backwards, headfirst, and under the surface. A big fish – face, belly, legs, toes last, and then gone. Just for a second and then up again with not even a gasp.

There was no shock or chill when I climbed down and in, up to my neck. I kept one hand on the ladder. Mrs Fletcher was maybe twenty yards away now, moving through the wobbling water.

Then I went straight in and right under. I wondered what the ducks thought of that. I went beyond time, escaped, magic. It's true that Lauren was with me then.

When I came up for air, Mrs Fletcher had grabbed hold of a big floating rubber ring stationed in the middle of the pond, a place to rest.

"How you doing?" she asked me.

"Fucking great," I told her, exhilarated. Almost forty and I still felt a thrill swearing in front of my friend's mum. She laughed. I stretched my legs so they were pointing straight down, and I was almost a bit disappointed that they didn't touch any weeds or fish or anything at all.

I stayed there by the rubber ring but I let go of it and leaned back, took a deep breath so my lungs would be full of air like armbands, and let my scalp sink into the water. I wiped the hair from my face, out of my eyes, made sure it was wet so it would stay stuck down. The stars were out, actually twinkling, a long long way away. I thought it was a shame that people had already spent so long going on about looking at the stars, the wonders of the universe, we are tiny flecks and all that.

"We are all in the pond," I said to Mrs Fletcher. "But some of us are looking at the stars." She made a little laughing-huff noise, and she probably looked up at the stars then, if she hadn't been looking already. I took another deep breath so I'd float a bit higher and I lifted one foot up to touch the gloopy underside of the rubber ring, to make sure I wasn't drifting off anywhere. Nothing reached up from the depths to grab me, and I didn't fall into the sky.

And then I go under again. Sounds are at once very close and far away. I cannot hear my own body. Lauren is here for as long as I hold my breath in the dark soft water. My eyes are closed too. What have I forgotten, about Lauren? I can't remember her voice and I don't have a recording. I don't want a recording. I try to think of one solid thing, one memory I can pick up and look at, and there is nothing. How cruel. Am I a fraud, to say

I loved her? But I remember walking and talking, and swimming and dancing. I know they all happened. I remember the car, when we crashed, and how she was shouting and then how she was quiet. I must have been screaming, because my throat was raw for days afterwards. That was all that was wrong with me, though. Not a fucking scratch on me. It wasn't my fault you know, officially and legally and in actual reality. But here I am, and where is Lauren? She is under the cold soft dark water, swimming, swimming with me. We are weightless in the slow dark, and there are unknown treasures just beyond our reach, and we move and glance and dream together of wordless pleasures. We are dancing, dancing, to put those pale, lost lilies out of mind.

Love! Love!

Carl walked over with this extraordinary pile, this seafood platter on a big silver dish – huge prawns in their armour nestled on the crushed ice, soft golden mussels inside their black shells, raggedy pale oysters all smooth and slurpy inside with chunks of lemon on top. He was grinning. Behind him Lucy carried five shots of absinthe in sherry glasses on a round black tray with a jug of water.

We were in the Fitzroy Tavern on a bank holiday Sunday and it was still quiet even though it was mid-afternoon. I was playing the early set so we were at a table right by the DJ booth, where my music was in two boxes – one big, one small – tucked under the decks along with our coats. I'd put on a compilation album to keep the speakers busy: John Lee Hooker was about to turn into The Moonglows.

"This is meta-food," said Lucy, stroking a prawn. Carl swilled his glass about a bit and sniffed it. Lucy poured a bit of water into her absinthe and I held mine up so she'd do the same for me. Then I sipped my pearly drink and watched Lucy, the best of all my best friends, pull the head and tail off that prawn, drag a nail along its roe-covered belly and suck the little black eggs from her fingers.

Then my boy Carl was talking to Stella, who hadn't seen him for a while and was glad of a fresh audience for her tales of last weekend, when she had gone to Southend with Jackson for

Jackson's grandma's 100th birthday at Jackson's mum's house. She'd waltzed with Jackson's stepdad round their front room, in their two-up-two-down terrace, yellowed all over from fag smoke and with cranberry glass in the cabinets. She'd watched as Jackson's niece, not quite two, had ambled straight into the garden pond – "I was holding two glasses of pink wine, I couldn't do a thing" – and later she had sat in the front room holding his grandma's downy hand.

And then Jackson's seven-year-old nephew had asked if he could draw Stella's picture. Which was sweet. He had already drawn Jackson in a big notebook, made Jackson look like Desperate Dan, basically. He was not an unskilled little artist. And he'd drawn his mum, Jackson's sister, who was all hair and toothy smile, also very sweet. He sat there looking at Stella, drew her hair (black), her legs (long) and her eyes (blue), then he added big boobies ("Is that what they're called when you're seven?") and then, between her legs, he scribbled a huge black bush.

"Cheeky shit!" Stella laughed. "It looked like Mr Messy, but without the smiley face."

Carl's face was scrunched up in delight and he shuddered with giggles.

"In the end the bush was bigger than me," Stella sighed.

Lucy was doing my easy-peasy DJing for me, putting on Alice Coltrane, "because no one ever in the history of civilisation has complained about hearing Alice Coltrane in a chi-chi north London pub on a hungover Sunday afternoon, you know, and no one ever will." Then she was chatting to Paulie, and they headed to the bar for more absinthe and to talk to Al and Joe and Jamie, who had just walked in. Stella was in the toilets, or maybe she was with Lucy at the bar.

So Carl snuggled up against me with the crossword. We were half-sitting, half-lying on the big leather sofa, sunlight faint through thick old glass, dirt between the floorboards, flowers blousy and wilting. We were quiet there together for a few still minutes. Once or twice Carl turned his head to touch his nose to my ear, or to my neck, or to rest his lips on my shoulder. There were people around and a messy night coming for us, but nothing yet to do except think *Romantic poem or scene* (5). *Existing only in bits and pieces* (11).

Three hours later the pub was properly packed. Franco was playing You Can Call Me Al and we were dancing on the tables. Stella grabbed my leg and held it up for the bass solo, slapped and popped the imaginary strings running down my thigh while I hung onto her shoulder, hopped on my other leg. Carl was doing the brass. I was sticky with absinthe. Then next, when I heard Kids In America starting, I was so excited that I just fell over like an ecstatic tim-berrrrrrr tree. Except that I didn't quite, because Lauren and Mandy and a few others were dancing right next to our table, and Mandy shouted "catch her!" and they lifted me and passed me along, right around the bar and rotating me, in a slow and cuddly crowdsurf. Long before I'd got to the first batch of "naaa naa na-na naaa" they'd delivered me softly back and upright to the table and I was baptised by good vibes. Seriously.

A man's head had appeared for a moment or two between my legs just as I was being gently spun back round towards my table. The eye contact we made had somehow been more happy than awkward. He was pretty. He had big dark eyes and a wonky nose. I went to the toilet a few songs after Kim, and as I came back out of the rickety door he was walking up the stairs. I backed into the bathroom, not thinking really about anything except his big wonky nose and his smiling face between my legs. What was especially nice is that he just smiled at me, laughed quietly like a tickled toddler, and walked straight in after me, stroked my cheek, kissed me. We circled round each other for a second and then I had my back against the door and he knelt in front of me, pulled my jeans open. The idea of him giving me head in the toilet was better than the head he actually gave me, but that was okay. He was giggly and slobbery and, Well, what gusto, what an appetite! I thought, He's really *relishing* this. He tasted delicious when I kissed him (of course) and he was straightforward and affectionate. He nuzzled me a little longer and then he left me alone for the rest of the night. So pretty.

The bar was still thronged, hot like it might be good for your bronchitis, and full of smiles. I got back in there and scanned about for Lucy. She was in the corner, doing that slowly-collapsing dance that Ally Sheedy does in The Breakfast Club – arms up and body shaking, and down to your knees and head to the floor and full-flop into the music. I still had blue-and-yellow knees from doing the same dance with her on Thursday. Carl was giving Paulie a shoulder-rub, sitting on a sofa in the quieter bit round the corner, but then he leapt up when they played California Uber Alles. That song always brings out the shouty man in him, and Lucy too was whooping, all big eyes and making revving-engine noises. Paulie stayed on the sofa, head back and smiling, the first sign that the night was drawing to a close even while it was peaking.

The doors were locked now and Stella was by the kitchen smoking a fag, talking to Lauren and Mandy. Millie in the football vest hugged me and gave me a blissful kiss, her sweaty face slipping across mine. I dipped my little finger into the little bag of pink MDMA that she cradled close between us like a candle, licked the sharp powder, imagined the powder-pink and the absinthe-green in my belly, a sorcerer's recipe.

"Come here!" Carl was yelling. He was on the bar, crouched down, his arms stretched out to me. I went in for a cuddle, into his soft wet neck, but he was pulling me up onto the bar, he wanted us dancing up there together. I couldn't do it. I thought I might slip, fall, smash my teeth, black my eye, damage myself too much. Embarrassing, stranded, frozen, hopeless. Carl took my arms, just above my elbows, and pulled me up, right up, until I was sitting on the bar. Then I grabbed onto him and he pulled again and I wobbled and we stood upright together between the beer levers and the curved metallic edge.

"Magic," he said, and we kissed, first a touch of lips and then a proper ridiculous open-mouth dive-in where your heads airlock together and you really just want to have sex. "That's my favourite kind of kiss," I told him. I liked them all, though.

Paulie had a congregation on his sofa and in the chairs around his table. Stella had her arms around Lauren and Lucy, who were curled either side of her on a wide, comfy chair. Joe and Mandy had four more absinthes, unwatered – one glass each and another lined up waiting. As they talked, fixed into a discussion, they would occasionally dip a forefinger into the glass and lick off the goo, like baby birds being fed or children with a bag of sherbet. Jamie moved and sat on Millie's lap when we walked over, so Carl and I had a chair to ourselves. I settled in sideways on the arm and he sat squarely down on my feet, his weight and his warmth on my toes.

It wasn't all that late, about one o'clock. There'd be a party at Al's house later, but that wasn't quite happening yet. We were enjoying a lull between chapters. And anyway the next stage might be to go home, fruity tea and duvet and cleaned teeth and Carl's smooth warm firm body next to mine.

Mandy passed us the spare absinthes. "We have spare absinthe," she said, proud. I leaned over and poured a glass of tap water from the jug on the table, no ice, and I drank it, steady gulps, before I started to sip the absinthe. Like sherry, in its sherry glass, but hotter and better.

Carl was talking to Paulie, being all earnest and important. "It's about the fun and loving each other, and the glorious universe we're all part of, and it's about being good to each other."

Lauren and Lucy, in sync, lifted their heavy, lovely heads, regarded my boyfriend with soft smiles. Jamie and Mandy were gazing, half laughing, half swooning at Carl.

And Carl noticed his audience, turned his head, his shoulders dropped back a bit. "What in life is more important than love and music and friends and dancing?"

"Fucking hippy," said Jamie, and then he pushed himself up like a pendulum, tick-tocked straight onto Carl and began to wriggle against Carl's leg like a horny dog with a new technique.

"Let's have a toast!" I shouted, my absinthe held up in the air. "A toast to friends and raving and the glorious universe!"

"Whoo!" yelled Stella.

"Ya-oo!" cried Lucy.

"Love! Love!" said Joe. "Love is all you need!"

And we drank, then looked around at each other. What to do next? And Paulie went for more drinks.

Almost everyone did go back to Al's that night, but I said to Carl, "Are you a bit tired?" and he said, "Are you?" and we set off home together, walking.

It was the end of May, warm and clear. We were on residential streets, wide and Victorian, solid houses and no one around, just a twenty-minute walk but with record boxes – we'd swap between the big and the little one. Carl began to sing, an old music-hall ditty, he reckoned, that he liked to sing to me like a lullaby for grown-ups.

"Tiddly winky winky winky, tiddly winky woo, I love you," he sang in my ear, very quietly at first. Shy, but he wanted to sing it.

"Tiddly winky winky winky, tiddly winky woo, love me too." At this point he went a bit Max Wall.

"I love you in the morning, I love you in the night, I love you in the evening when the stars are shining bright," which they were.

"Tiddly winky winky winky, tiddly winky woooo, I looove you (without your bra on), I love you (without your pants on), I love you (without your wig on), I loooooove you."

By the end of the ditty he was two or three metres ahead on the pavement, facing me, moving backwards in a slow jig. His feet occasionally kicked one way or the other, and his elbows were poking out. And then he stopped, with knees bent, arms spread, small record box in one hand, shoulders in a shrug, head to one side, eyebrows up in a croon. And I stopped too, and looked at him and smiled, the tired smile of a tired parent.

We swapped boxes again, so he had the bigger one, the one which would bash against your knee and give you a wooden-leg walk. There wasn't a car or a dog-walker or a night-bus on the streets. Just me and Carl. He carried the big box the rest of the way, up our front steps and into our flat. "Give me that," he said as we got through the door, and he put both boxes gently by the stereo, the little one neat and straight in front of the big one.

"No more booze," I said. "Let's have fruit tea and a bath." Carl went to the kettle and mugs, I went to turn on the taps. Sitting on the side of the bath, I pulled off my clothes, shuffled out of my jeans, didn't unlace my shoes, just pushed them off with my heels, left it all collapsed there on the floor like I'd been dematerialised, and I watched the water thunder out, just the hot tap. Then the cold, and watching and listening, and I slipped in with the taps still running. Is there anything better than a bath?

"Shall I wash your back, darling?" Carl asked me. Two blackberry-and-nettle teas on top of the toilet seat. Then "fucking hell, you do look good" and an upside-down kiss, his hand stroking from my cheek and down my neck, between my breasts and down between my legs, around my thigh, his face sinking into me a little, just against my ear.

I wanted the bath to myself. Carl sat on the floor against the radiator, a towel across his knee and another folded behind his head. He was humming that Tiddly song, very slowly, and watching me. From where he sat he could see just my face and my legs. He didn't wash my back but sometimes he would lean forwards and stroke down my leg, and sometimes he would lean over and take a sip of his tea. My toes reached the taps, one hot toe and one cold toe, made squeaky noises.

"What are you thinking about?" he asked me, one word after another.

"I'm thinking about men and cock and not being dead," I said. My arms were up above my head, fingers exploring my damp hair and sweaty scalp.

"I'd love to fuck you now," he told me. He had such a sweet voice. "You're beautiful."

"I'm tired."

I am special and I will not die, I thought. I will keep the end at bay with a constant shuffling of men and possibilities. To be in love would be some kind of death.

I looked at Carl, took an inventory of his face, of him. His hair was pale gold-brown and tufty, his skin was lightly freckled. His cheekbones were so delicate but he had this thick, serious brow. His T-shirt was baggy around the neck so I could see a bit of his collarbone. His big bottom lip was sucked in under his front teeth. His eyes were fixed somewhere near my feet.

The bath felt cold. I thought about putting some more hot water in but then I pulled the plug out, just hooked my toe around the chain and tugged.

Good Solid
Obliterating Fuck

I met Proust, more or less, on the train from Aberdeen to London in 2001. He wasn't called Marcel, as far as I know, and he was better-looking than Proust, but he was dreamy and kind and slim, with these long elegant fingers and soft high cheekbones, and he talked in long beautiful sentences where I would forget by the time he got to the end, got to where the full stop might be, what he had started with and what the actual point of the sentence could be; who is doing the thing that is being done in this sentence, and when were they doing it, and what does it relate to, why are you telling me? And I didn't mind the forgetting, because it's not a police statement, you know, it's a story.

I'd been dozing when the man sat down opposite me, because I do tend to fall asleep on trains. I was snuggled up and softly snoozing. I dreamt of my old schoolfriends Lisa and Janey. They were sitting across the table from me and it felt familiar as well as a bit strange because I hadn't seen them in years, and what had we missed? We chatted for a while and they invited me to join them on a daytrip to the seaside – faraway tides and long beaches, and a very good crabshack apparently. We could take some more time to catch up, update biographical details, remember habits and expressions, remember how much we like each other and why. I didn't want to go, but I was glad to be asked.

In the dream, Lisa was wearing this white dress that she used to love, off-white really, secondhand but pristine, soft, cotton, buttons, pockets, easy, simple. The feeling of it. I would like to hold onto that dress like a Linus blanket, like a child with her mother's skirt, like a lover in a cliche gripping the sheet while she gets a really good solid obliterating fuck.

Then the man sat down, diagonally opposite me, and that woke me up although I didn't move. He gave me a quick nod. He was handsome. I gave a little nod in return. The handsome Prousty man sat down opposite me on the train. I liked that, and I dozed off again. And then the man was in my dream, I think, although I'm not certain.

Next time I woke up there was a bit of dribble at the corner of my mouth. The handsome man didn't seem to have noticed, but then he shuffled sideways out of his seat, stood up, and looked at me.

"Do you want anything from the buffet car?"

Well, now, isn't that an old-fashioned term for it? Buffet car.

I would love a cup of tea, I told him, straight in, as if he offered me a brew every morning. I didn't mean to whisper but I did because my lips were dry and my throat was claggy from sleeping.

And when he came back with a cup of tea and a Kitkat I found it borderline creepy, because I hadn't said anything about wanting a chocolate bar, but the truth is that I also really fancied a Kitkat, so there we were. I felt, for a second, as if I knew him.

"I was at the festival too," he told me.

Ah, so he was. The film festival I'd been at for the past three days, working, shmoozing.

"I'm not quite awake," I told him. "But I knew I recognised you from somewhere."

"We were at the same screening of Beau Travail. Sitting on the same row, I think."

"Oh my god," I remembered the film, the wonderful film. "Those men, those bodies."

"Those bodies," he sighed. "And isn't it compelling, those bodies moving in the heat, moving in space, not outer space-space, of course, I mean in the Djibouti desert-space, moving and sweating, almost like synchronised swimmers! And there was something so exquisite and so heartbreaking as well as sexy, utterly sexy, about the dynamics between them, seeing them helpless really as they get tangled up in those pulsing rivalries."

"I love a bit of male rivalry," I told him. "Especially when it's under a female gaze."

"Because that makes a nice change, you mean?"

"Oh, I suppose so. That's quite petty, isn't it? A pathetic sort of equality."

"It's fair enough, though. No pun intended. And she is an amazing director."

"Thanks for the tea."

I offered him money, he didn't want money, he said I could get the next one if I liked and then he pulled a tiny face, a shy little grimace, because he realised there was something cheesy about mentioning the next cup of tea we have together, something he hadn't really intended about suggesting that we will have other cups of tea together, just the two of us.

"What is the French Foreign Legion, exactly?" I was thinking about the film again, those men. "I just imagine it as pirates but on land."

"And a bit like the circus," he said. "In the sense that you go off and join it."

"'He went off and joined the French Foreign Legion.' When was that a saying? It was a saying, wasn't it?"

He thought about that for a minute, this handsome man with his delicate features. "I feel like there was a time when young men just disappeared, just upped and left. And what would you say? What do you say about that?"

"Women join the circus, men get the French Foreign Legion?"

"You're talking as if that's a bad deal for women, again, but I'm not sure it is."

"Well, that's fair enough."

He started humming, Nellie the Elephant packed her trunk and said goodbye to the circus.

"When did these phrases start?" I asked. I was relaxed and my mind was noodling about. "When did they go away?"

"Nowadays we all know that no one's actually joined the circus. They're just divorced somewhere with two kids, or they're in prison."

"No shame in either of those things," I told him.

And he agreed, or at least he nodded. He was having a think. "I don't want to be lazy," he said.

"Do you live in London?"

"No, no, I live in Paris."

"Ah, lovely."

"Although I'm actually flying to Milan in the morning."

"Well, now you're showing off."

"I am rather jetset."

"Do you speak Italian?"

"Ovviamente parlo Italiano," he said.

"Is that Italian, or pisstake Italian?"

"How rude." He was smiling at me, not in a pisstake way.

"Sorry. I am ignorante of the romantic languages."

"That's actually the right word, in Italian. Ignorante means ignorant. So you're not as ignorante as you think."

"Ha! I'm more romantico than I realised."

He looks down as if I've said the wrong thing.

"Or would it be romantica?"

"Romantico," he said. And then he said, "Do you think we're flirting?"

"I've no idea," I told him, which was true.

That shut us both up but it didn't feel uncomfortable, or not to me anyway. I had a slurp of my tea, which had some very very small bits of Kitkat floating in it, evidence of the dunking I'd been doing, and the tastes and the textures were so slight and so familiar, the tiny blobs of fat and the sugary soggy fragments of wafer, and the whole miniature experience blossomed into a great reassuring flower with me curled up inside it like a flower fairy, and then I imagined the flower fairy, who was me, sitting on the floor in front of the easy chair where my grandma was sitting, and she had a cigarette burning in the ashtray next to her (this at a time when the smell of a Lambert & Butler cigarette was associated with half my family, was no bad thing and was certainly not some bearer of feckless doom and death) and she had a rag in her hand, a torn strip of cotton from an old sheet or something, and she was putting my hair into rags which means she was winding a segment of my damp-from-the-bath hair around each rag and then winding the remainder of the rag back around the hair and tying it at the top, moving across my scalp with gentle attention and method, pausing sometimes to take a drag on her cigarette but mainly leaving it to burn away in the ashtray, and in a little while it will all be done and I will look like a Victorian child, and then she'll take the rags out, starting where she began, and then I'll have soft ringlets. And I will be gloriously dipped in the playfulness and lovingness and sparkling idleness of my grandma.

"I think it's probably okay to be lazy," I told the handsome man, stirring in my seat and actually, I realised, trying to get more comfy because I was in danger of dozing off again.

"You're probably right," he said. "Again."

I laughed because he was being sardonic or whatever, but also he was right about me being right. I am frequently right.

I looked out the window for the first time in a while, at the low grey northern sky, daydreaming a bit, about those hard smooth battered torsos in Beau Travail, imagining how they would taste, if I licked them, how they would feel underneath me, on top of me. I was very relaxed with this strange man. When I looked over at him again, he was listening to something on his headphones and looking quite dreamy himself.

"What you listening to?" I sort-of mouthed this at him and tapped one ear.

He took the headphones off. I'd interrupted him entirely.

"Steppin' Out," he said. "An old song by Joe Jackson."

"He's not one of the Jacksons?"

"Nope. A different kind of Jackson." The handsome man leaned over the table and put his headphones on me which for a second was just slightly thrilling. Then he skipped back to the start of the song and I listened. It was good. I recognised it, maybe. It was dreamy, too, with lyrics about two people on a night out, stepping into the night, he sang, stepping into the light.

"What does this sound like? My Sharona? Devo? The Go-Go's?" I was careful not to shout, with the headphones on.

He shrugged and nodded because, yep, it probably sounded like all of those. I kept listening, looked out the window, with Joe Jackson sounding a bit melancholy but also hopeful, and like he's in the early 1980s and probably in New York, a bit bookish, a bit cocainey, quite well groomed, wears pastels.

The handsome man opposite me was talking, and I couldn't really hear him until I took off the headphones and he repeated, "Is it a shame, do you think, that everything reminds us of something else?"

"Does this song remind you of anything?"

"It reminds me of being a kid and thinking that grown-ups are glamorous."

"What else?"

"Well, it reminds me of a feeling. It reminds me of my parents having parties."

"Did they play this song at their parties?"

"I don't know, but I feel like they did."

"Good enough," I told him. "Good enough. Where did you live when you were little?"

"In a semi in south London. Dulwich. Mum, dad, younger sister. My uncle lived nearby."

"Nice."

"It was nice."

"Nice to have family living nearby. Your uncle, I mean."

"It was. It meant a lot to me, when I was little, having him close. But then he had a falling-out with the rest of the family. Which was my fault, really."

I settled in my seat even more when he said that, because I knew he was about to tell me a story and because if there's something that makes you feel guilty in a complicated way, I want to hear about it.

"Every week, or sometimes twice a week," he began, "I'd be allowed to go off on my own to visit my uncle. That is, I'd be allowed to cross the main road near our house and cut through the park to get to his house."

"How old were you?"

"I'm not sure. Eight or nine, maybe."

"So that was quite an adventure, at that age."

"I realise now that my mum and my uncle – her brother – must have agreed on the times I'd go and visit. So she'd wave me off, and he would be waiting at his house for me to arrive, he'd either be at the door or it'd be on the latch so I could saunter straight in. My mum probably watched me cross the road and then phoned him to tell him that I'd be there in ninety seconds. A domestic operation of military precision."

"Loosening the apron strings, just a bit."

"Yes. She softly chucked me over to him and he softly caught me. And I used to love his house. He would sit with me at the kitchen table there and chop up fruit with a stumpy little knife, an apple or a pear or a banana, and we'd eat the pieces together, one at a time, and talk – I mean, I suppose we talked, I can't remember properly, but I remember the kitchen, and the colours in there, it was a rich blue, the kind of blue you want to stick your finger into, a heavenly blue, and the smell of his house was heavenly too. Our house didn't smell of anything, not that I remember, but my uncle's house would be alive, alive inside your nose."

He laughed at this phrase – 'alive inside your nose' – and I did as well but only a quick laugh so as not to interrupt him. I felt like a fin-de-siecle psychotherapist, and I was enjoying it.

"It smelt soft and slightly sweet, in his house. Like someone had been crushing and toasting hazelnuts in there, maybe a couple of days ago, and then the windows had been open for a few hours in the late morning on a warm day. It smelt like how hospitals would smell if they wanted people to heal faster. If shops smelt like that, no one would buy anything because they'd already be completely content. If schools smelt like that, the children would learn faster, their times tables but also how the soil feels when the grass pushes through it, and how the ant feels when it's climbing that grass and the blade swings and bounces gently under its ant weight."

"Under its ant weight," I said. Enjoying even more this unexpected and pleasantly doolally turn in the conversation.

"And my uncle smelled good too, he wore a bit of aftershave I think or he used a nice soap or washing powder. And sometimes we would sit on his sofa, which was a long stylish sofa with a long stylish coffee table in front of it. I do remember some of what we talked about, actually, on that sofa. I do remember him playing me records and telling me about the bands he liked, and I'd tell him which songs I liked. We had a little listening club. I was into Soft Cell but I wasn't sure about Redskins, and he'd play me a song and get me to listen to a particular bit that he loved, over and over. Ba-doo, ba-doo-doo. And he'd make me a cup of tea, something I considered at that point to be very grown-up, almost as grown-up as a glass of wine."

The handsome man looked at my plasticky-paper cup of tea, finished now on the little table between us, and at his cup, which was empty too.

"I don't think I was exactly aware of the judgements and opinions of adults, as a child, but I knew that my uncle liked me, and that he thought I was funny and clever, and I took this to be a reassuring indication that I would turn out alright. I was starting to become aware of the ongoingness of things, the fact that if I liked something now, I might like it later. That if I was okay now, I might be okay later. Does that make sense?"

"Yes, of course it does."

"The house I lived in then is still there. My uncle's house is still there. But I did fuck up, and I also feel like if I fucked up then, I'll fuck up again."

I wanted to know how the handsome man had fucked up. I waited for him to tell me.

"One morning, I went round to my uncle's house without letting anyone know I was going out. I woke up, and I wanted to see him. It was a Sunday morning, and I don't know what had happened but I woke up feeling unfinished and alone and I wanted to see my lovely uncle. I just walked out of the house. Over the road, very very careful even though there were no cars in sight. I crossed the park and knocked on his door and it didn't occur to me that he might not want his young nephew visiting early on a Sunday morning. I knocked and I heard noises inside, and music, and even then I don't think it occurred to me that, oh, maybe I shouldn't be here. Maybe he has other things to do. Other things to do on a Sunday morning."

I tried to imagine the handsome man, aged eight or nine. It was quite easy.

"Adults notice things about you that you haven't noticed yourself yet. When you're on the inside, and this is your first time around, you don't know what you are. You know you're not your mum or your dad or your sister. I did think I was my uncle, that's what I was realising, and this seemed a good thing. I liked him so much.

"When he opened the door that morning he was disheveled and wide-eyed. We might know what that means, now, especially on a Sunday morning. But I didn't know then. I don't think I even realised anything was different to my usual Tuesday afternoon visit, or not until I got inside, into the front room, where three other men were sitting, disheveled and wide-eyed and delighted to see me. It was, as I remember it, as though an extremely sweet and slightly shy puppy had ambled into the room. 'Oh look! Hello sweetheart!', they said, and 'Oh my god, the cuteness!' That's the phrase that stuck in my head: oh my god, the cuteness.

"He introduced me to these three men as his nephew, and they wanted a name, and they asked how old I was and would I like a glass of pop and I was just the most delightful thing they'd ever seen. Oh my god, the cuteness. They were elegant and exciting, fully formed men having so much fun and no one to tell them off, no one they had to ask for permission. One of them had blond curls, almost corkscrew curls. I could hardly bear to imagine ever being so comfortably and beautifully myself. I wonder what they look like now, where they are now. One of them wasn't wearing a top and I was thrilled, enthralled, by his bare chest. I was thrilled and enthralled that I was allowed to have a good look at it. I was probably staring, because he laughed and said, 'Do you like my pecs?' and my uncle made a strange little warning sound, a little tone from the back of his throat. And I wanted to nuzzle right into that man's chest, I wanted to put my face into it and I wanted to disappear into him like a little blob of mercury into a big blob of mercury.

"'Does your mum know you're here?' my uncle asked me. She did not, of course, so I shook my head. And all that happened next was that my uncle put on his shoes and got his door keys and said to me, 'Come on, we're going back over to your house. Your mum'll be worried.' And he took my hand, and I probably didn't say a word, and the three men said 'Seeya!' and 'Goodbye!' and 'Lovely to meet you, young man!' and off I went back over the road with my uncle. He didn't come in, he didn't even come to the door, he just watched and made sure I went inside.

"Except as we crossed the road he said, as if it wasn't very important, something like, 'There are things your mum and dad don't want to know.' It felt like a little puzzle to work out, but also I knew that what he meant was, 'Don't mention this to your mum and dad.' I wasn't at all clear, though, about what I shouldn't mention.

"And I was so pleased to have met these three friends of my uncle's, and so proud that they had liked me, and so delighted by this new sentence – 'oh my god, the cuteness!' – that I told my mum all about it. There was nothing bad to tell, it was all wonderful, these three glamorous and smiling men who approved of me so heartily.

"And my dad was there too and he was furious. I didn't know why and I still don't know really, except of course for the mundane dull-dull-as-fuck theory that he could see his only son turning out a bit queer and he didn't want me hanging out with any happy gay queer gay men. So I stopped going to my uncle's on Tuesday afternoons, and I don't think he came round to our house anymore either. I saw him at the shops, a few months later, and he looked like he was about to walk over and talk to me, but I looked down at the ground, totally blanked him. I didn't have the sense or the decency to know what to do, I was flummoxed by the whole situation. Kids are shit, aren't they? I didn't even ask my parents about it. Kids are shit. And I never saw my uncle again. He was dead, four years later. Out riding his bike, hit by a car. Killed instantly, I was told. Although I've become rather suspicious of how often people are apparently killed instantly."

"Oh fucking hell," is what I said in response to all this.

"And now I live in Paris, glamorous and friendly and successful, and I am a happy gay queer gay man."

"Your uncle would be entirely delighted," I said, trying not to put a that's-alright-then lid on his story.

The handsome man smiled at me, in agreement. He breathed in, soft and deep, then he breathed out again. "You were asleep, when I sat down."

"I was dreaming."

"What were you dreaming about?"

"I was dreaming about two women I haven't seen for years, women I was good friends with at school. We were chatting. They were going to the seaside and they invited me to go with them."

"And did you go?"

"I didn't quite fancy it."

"You might have had fun."

"I'm sure I would've. But the dream had already moved on, I was dreaming about things and fabrics and distant years, and how good it feels to have a really good solid obliterating fuck."

He shifted in his seat a little, but he didn't look away from me. And he smiled again. The smile wasn't bestowing anything on me, it was simply a happy reaction. So I'd checked, and it was okay to say 'good solid obliterating fuck' to this handsome man.

"Where did you come from?" I asked him. Then, to clarify, "Did you get on at Aberdeen?"

"My seat was in the next carriage, and it was near the toilet, and the toilet was oozing chemical shit smells and I was not into it."

"Eugh."

"Yes. Eugh. So I got my bag and I moved. And I thought, Ideally there'll be a seat at a table, and no one else there except for a woman who is fast asleep."

"That sounds weirder than you meant it to."

"I knew it would sound a bit weird."

"Tell me about your mum."

"No," he said, softly. "Don't get me started."

"It's true, you really can talk when you get going."

"I can do other things too," he said, and then he smiled at me and I felt comfortably wildly alive right there.

"Oh, well now we are flirting."

"I think I might be offering, rather than flirting."

I took a good look at him. At his face, first, and then at the way he was sitting. He had one hand, his left hand, resting on the table, slightly towards me, and he was leaning back in more of a repose than a slouch, elegant and louche, with his face relaxed and still, even more so compared to the speeding whizzing whooshing hills outside the window. It's true, I'm delaying telling you what happened next, which is that we talked about bodies and sex and terror.

He'd told me, I thought, that he has sex with men, and that made me relax because that meant we had something in common. No, I'm joking. It made me relax because I didn't have to worry too much about whether he wanted to have sex with me, a woman, or indeed whether I wanted to have sex with him.

So now he asked me, "What do you think about when you think about sex?"

"Weight. Heft. Heaviness," I told him. "Being banged."

"Being banged?" He didn't seem entirely impressed by the idea.

"I know. Fucked into oblivion."

"Okay."

"That good solid obliterating fuck."

"Okay. I'm getting a hard-on. I mean, I think it's alright to tell you that, but also I'm thinking about all the other possibilities. Apart from being obliterated, I mean."

"I panic at the other possibilities."

"You don't have to be right about anything, you know. You don't need to draw a manual. You don't even have to enjoy it."

"But I'd like to enjoy it, on balance."

"What would you enjoy? What would you like?"

"To be stroked. Stroked and banged and squashed and held tight."

"What if you take the weight away?"

"The wait?"

"The heaviness. The heft. What if you get rid of the big hefty bloke who's obliterating you?"

When he said this I looked at his skinny body.

"If I take that away then I get stroked and banged and I expand."

The train was zooming past gardens, long green back gardens, we must have been somewhere around York or Doncaster or even further by now, and I saw a man by a trampoline, no top on, jeans, dancing, light on his feet. He was dancing, performing, for someone out of my sight. A glimpse and then he was gone.

"You expand?"

"Like Violet Beauregarde, the purple little girl in Willy Wonka's chocolate factory. All my atoms are jiggling and I expand."

"Do you float away like Violet Beauregarde?"

"No. And is it too weird to use a small fictional child to illustrate my sexual desires?"

"She's not even a very likeable small fictional child."

"I don't float away, anyway. I loom and I conquer."

"Do you actually *do* anything? Do you do anything for the hefty man, I mean, in return for all this stroking and banging?"

"Ha! No. I enjoy it. I'm busy expanding, looming, conquering."

I shifted in my seat, like a schoolboy with an erection. He was watching me, and he seemed to very much approve of me. I looked around, just for a second, almost hoping someone was eavesdropping.

"None of it is good enough," I said. "I mean, almost never. And it's not that I'm handing out scores, it's more that I want to be connected inside the obliteration, I want no edges, I want to be squidged together and crying and screaming and gentle and, you know, a ruler of worlds, an adventurer into squelching realms."

"Squelching realms," he said.

"Yes," I said. "Yes."

I looked at him and remembered a line from a poem I'd read recently: *Hard and moist and moaning.* It was suddenly extremely easy to imagine this handsome man all hard and moist and moaning. It seemed an injustice in the world that he was not, right then and there, hard and moist and moaning.

"It is good, isn't it," I said, "to have someone want to fuck you in a way that is somehow more detailed, because they've properly noticed you."

"Yes, it is," he said, and his smile was so wide and his eyes actually did sparkle.

"And it's good to be stuffed and demented and alive," I said. I was feeling silly and great, wide awake. "How does this work?" I asked him. "When does it really get good?"

He was listening to me and he looked wistful. Simple as that, he looked wistful. And he really did look a bit like Proust, I thought. From a different time, and so elegant. But then he looked a bit like Buster Keaton too, Buster Keaton when he was very young and very beautiful. This man wasn't quite so beautiful, but nearly. Not far off.

Then he leaned forward, and spoke with clear soft syllables, like he was quoting a film or passing on a message: "It's like you woke up and I started dreaming."

I didn't know then, and I haven't learned since, what to do with something unexpected and precious. Do you even recognise it? Is it better not to?

It was just about getting dark outside, and soon we were heading past blocks of flats and scrubby trees into central London. I wanted to know where he was staying tonight and whether he might want to join me in a hotel bar somewhere near the station, for a cocktail or two.

"Here we are," he said, just as the conductor announced that we were arriving at King's Cross. He passed my bag down from the overhead shelf and I put on my coat and we moved down the carriage, the handsome man just behind me, protective really, and we stepped out, off the train, into the night, into the light.

Lunch

The tablecloth is thick white cotton. Two wine glasses and cloth napkins, the sun shining in and everything crisp and sparkling. Frank is looking at the menu. He suggested the noisy noodle place on Greek Street but I didn't want noisy noodles so we left before they took our order and we came here. The doorman smiled and said hello as we walked in. This restaurant is part of a hotel, in the middle of the city, expensive but not completely wanky.

Frank is sitting with his lovely face, right there. I used to imagine chatting to another colleague and mentioning Frank, in passing, describing his face as exquisite. "Frank is exquisite-looking," I'd say, and cause a little stir around the office. I never said it though, out loud.

There are small wrinkles in front of Frank's ears, because his face is drooping. He has brown eyes. He's wearing a soft wool suit and shiny shoes.

"Everything is good here," I tell him. "Well, maybe everything except the snails and bacon."

I've already decided, I'm having the beetroot and curd and barley. No wine because it's lunchtime. And in a bit of a hurry please because we want time for pudding too.

Frank is looking around, leaning back in his chair.

"This could be our place," he tells me. Then he smiles. "You look really well, Annie."

"I'm happy."

"The new job suits you."

"Yep. How are you?"

"I'm alright. A bit surprised still."

"Had you talked about it?"

"Yes, vaguely. I didn't think it would happen so quickly."

"Well, you know how it works."

"Yes, I know how it works."

I look at him and he keeps talking.

"I thought it might happen in a year or two. If we stayed together that long."

"How many weeks is she?"

"Twenty. Twenty-two. It was the last time we had sex, actually." A little laugh.

"Is she okay?"

"She's over the moon."

"You'll love it too, I bet, once you have an actual baby. You'll be a good dad."

"Thanks. Thanks. Do you want children?"

"I don't know. I'd definitely like a shag."

"But you wouldn't want a boyfriend," he says. "I mean you wouldn't want a boyfriend who felt trapped."

"The two of you talked about it, didn't you?"

"I thought it would take months for her to get pregnant."

"And you thought she couldn't get pregnant standing up. Or on Thursdays."

"Don't be clever."

"But I am clever."

"Snails and bacon," he tells the waiter.

"And I'll have the beetroot and curd. And shall we share a side salad?" I look at Frank.

"What about the broccoli?"

"Broccoli. Yep. And a jug of tap water please."

"I'll have a small glass of house red too," Frank says. "You want one?"

"No thanks."

"I can't drink at home."

"Why not?"

"Well, I can, I just don't like doing it. Kelly isn't drinking at all and I don't like drinking on my own."

"But I'm not drinking right now either."

"Well, that's true. I've got this meeting after lunch, though, and it'll be better if I've had a glass of wine first."

"If we were in France now we'd both just be getting pissed."

"Or if we were in America in the 1950s."

"Or if we were just alkies."

"Or if we were in the music industry in the 90s."

"Then we'd be having chang in the toilets and drinking booze because we couldn't manage solids."

"Which would be a shame because the food here looks really good." He is eyeing the huge pie being shared by the two men at the next table.

"See if you still think that when your snails arrive."

"I only ordered those to spite you."

"Brilliant. Well done."

Right then his snails and bacon arrive, and his nose wrinkles.

"It does look a bit strange," I say. "It'll taste good though."

"Hmm."

"You can start, don't worry, mine will be here in a minute."

"You want a bit?"

"No thanks. I seem to have developed an allergy to shellfish. Do you think snails count as shellfish?"

"I doubt it," he says. "Don't risk it though, eh?"

My food arrives and Frank takes a slice of my beetroot. Then he says, "I know a lot of people at the moment who are breaking up, people with kids I mean. Lots of my friends."

"One thing at a time."

"Yes."

"I've only met Kelly once or twice."

"She's good. She can take care of herself."

"And a baby."

"And a baby, yes."

"While you're breadwinning."

"While I'm stuck in meetings."

"You could leave your job and stay at home with the baby while Kelly works."

"Excellent idea. I'd love that. Shit and puke and screaming."

"And that's just you."

"I envy you. Doing what you want to do."

"Oh yes. Well, it is pretty enviable. Life is good."

"You haven't got yourself a young man though?"

"No, no young men. Just me."

"Just you."

"Do you want to hear stories of clammy drunken trysts with work experience boys?"

"No. No thanks."

I tear a piece of crusty white bread, stick it in some butter, put a bit of salt on it. Frank watches me.

"Maybe you'll be pregnant this time next year." Suddenly he looks like he's going to cry.

"Maybe." My napkin is still folded, next to my plate. "How's the office?"

"Pretty great. Trevor has left, finally."

"He was the only real pain in the arse there. I might have stayed if he'd fucked off a bit sooner."

"I know. Well, I'm glad he's gone. The new bloke is lovely, and really good."

"Result."

"It's a happy situation all round."

"And you're enjoying those snails, after all."

"I am," he says, with this beautiful daft smile on his face.

Then Frank has to go for his meeting. No time for pudding.

"Let me pay."

"No, I'll get it, that's fine."

"You can treat us next time."

We head up the street, side by side, up to the revolving door of his office building.

"I'll see you at Julie's party next month maybe."

"Yes, definitely." He hugs me then he tucks his hands in his pockets. I turn to leave before he does.

The sun is still out. I dig out my ipod and head to the newsagents on the corner for a strawberry Cornetto.

Half a Point
for a Good Guess

My friend Inga got married in a wood a few miles outside Reykjavik, not because she wanted a cool wedding abroad but because she is Icelandic. Leo and Cathy and I flew over together from London. When the pilot spoke over the tannoy, Leo said, "Wow, it's Inga flying the plane!" Inga's was the only Icelandic voice we knew, and there we were surrounded by people who sounded like her. We had seen Inga only once or twice since we left college, since she moved back home. I had come to the wedding to demonstrate that we are still friends, that friends are for life, and because I wanted to dance and sing at an Icelandic wedding and see the midnight sun.

The hotel was swanky and right in the centre. We had a room each – grown-ups – and a swig each of vodka from Cathy's minibar before we set off to the wedding. Then we got lost on the way to the ceremony and the taxi driver was no help. Cathy had the address carefully copied down onto a scrap of paper but he just looked at it blankly. He called his cab office while Leo sat watching in the front seat with a calm-under-pressure face on and Cathy and I sat in the back, applying lipstick and exchanging comedy-panic gurns.

"Okay," said the driver, and we set off again. Neat, empty roads with a few neat, bright houses. Green grass and black rocks and blue sky. I love weddings. But then we stopped again, pulled into a layby, and the driver was back on his radio.

"Can you call a bride ten minutes before she's due to get married?" I said. "She could give us directions." We didn't know anyone else who'd be at the wedding.

"It's a quandary," said Leo. "A modern dilemma. Maybe a text is okay."

"No!" said Cathy. "We'll find it!"

The driver was nodding and grunting into the radio, and then we were off. We pulled up outside a little wooden church, but Inga wasn't having a church wedding. "She's not a god sort of a person," Leo told the driver. I nipped out just in case and had a look, put my head round the door, in the middle of the ceremony. The guests looked around with polite confusion, as if an errant hen had just clucked into their wedding. I smiled at the bride – not Inga – then dashed back to the car.

"Drive!" I said, all giddy. "Drive!" As if I'd just robbed a bank. We headed up the hill and there it was, like a big municipal scout hut, a one-storey wooden building, white, with a long porch. A ruddy man in a shiny sky-blue suit grinned as we got out of the taxi all frantic and faffy, confused by the krona and annoying the driver.

"I speak English!" boomed the ruddy man, a man born to host. He was wearing a purple cravat. He reminded me of the Simon Callow character in Four Weddings And A Funeral, but about twenty years younger and Icelandic.

"Plenty of time," said the mind-reading, ruddy man. It was two minutes to three but everyone was milling about and there was no sign of Inga or the groom – Magnus, he was called. Magnus! We'd met him once when Inga brought him to London to meet her old college friends.

The ceremony wasn't for half an hour, apparently, and it was a little walk away. Thirty or forty of us made our way through the woods, following blue ribbons tied to branches which led us to a clearing. It was hot and the woods were shady, everything soft and nature-made. Inga and Magnus were already there in the clearing, sitting on a fallen-down tree, talking with their heads dipped and eyes lifted. She looked amazing, and though I have never seen a bride who didn't look amazing, every time I see a friend get married I am amazed afresh by how amazing she looks. Every time. The three of us waved and she zoomed right over, hugs and kisses and such straightforward pleasure to see an old friend so happy.

A man who very nearly had pointy ears and who certainly had twinkly eyes – Chief Elf we called him – led the ceremony. The three of us stood quietly and listened carefully, not understanding a word, laughing gently when everyone else did, keeping quiet when everyone else did, good children at morning assembly. My high heels were sinking into the ground, so I leaned forward a bit, lifted the weight off one foot and then the other. A toddler in a three-piece suit was entranced by Inga and Magnus as they exchanged vows and rings. He was in an upright coma, bottom lip hanging. At the end, everyone clapped. Cathy gave a whistle, Leo wiped a tear.

We were stragglers on the way back to the scout hut, talking about the ceremony ("ace dress. She's so glam") and stroking trees, squeezing frothy blossoms to find out how they smelled on our hands. Cathy took off her shoes and padded along in her blunt bare feet but the ground looked too prickly for me. Leo was wearing a beige suit, crumply, with a bright blue tie and a silver tie pin. He looked just right, you could trust him with anything.

"I'm hungry," he said.

"We should eat before we drink too much."

"Feed me," said Cathy. "Feed me and booze me."

Three long tables were set for dinner, and people were checking the seating plan and settling into chairs when we got there. Purple and white flowers were in small round pots, silver cutlery shone like someone's auntie had been up all night with the Brasso and I could smell that welcoming red wine smell from the jugs that sat along the table. Cathy was to my left, and Leo to her left, and on my right there was a gravedigger. I introduced myself and pulled details slowly out of him. He was from Newcastle, he had a scar running down underneath one eye, and he told me about digging graves in Iceland, in the light summer months and the dark winter months.

"You use a JCB in the bigger graveyards," he told me. "But you do it all by hand in the smaller ones."

"And digging graves in the dark, all winter!"

"We have lights. And people just leave you alone."

He didn't really want to talk about digging graves in the dark all winter. His wife, Pála, the reason he had come to Iceland, was no-nonsense beautiful, with fat lips and pink cheeks and clear grey eyes. She explained the menu to me from across the table, pronouncing the Icelandic words slowly and softly, and translating it into English with little asides – "Kalkúnasalat, a chicken salad, Inga's mother made it, with lots of thyme. Plokkfiskur, fish stew, fresh I bet, very local. It will be delicious."

"Nearly everything is imported here," her husband said. His key fact about the menu. "There's not much native food. Just fish and yoghurt."

"And salty liquorice," I added, because I love salty liquorice and had bought some earlier.

"Most of the butter's imported," he said, appalled, not listening to me.

Next to Pála was a woman a few years younger than us, with a small child on her lap. The child held a piece of bread in one fist and was putting butter on it with his fingers.

"Okay you," the woman was saying, smiling into his hair. She spoke English but her accent sounded Icelandic. "You making a good mess there?"

"Yes!" he said, and carried on. The woman began to talk to Pála in Icelandic. I didn't understand why she'd spoken to her son in English. The child wriggled out of her lap and headed off down the table but she didn't look round, just kept chatting. He was offering his buttery hands to the people sitting a few seats down and they cooed and grinned like they were delighted by the offer, even as they leaned away.

Then Pála began to sing, not loud or showy, looking at her copy of a booklet that we each had in front of us. The woman next to her began to sing too, and before they'd got to the second line it seemed the whole room had joined in. Except for me and Leo and Cathy. I mouthed along a little, the way I might for hymns at a funeral, and then Pála leaned over and showed me which song in the booklet we were singing, what line we were up to. It was in Icelandic but this guidance helped – I joined in, had had enough wine that I didn't feel too worried about my phonetic singing, the fact that I must have sounded like a badly programmed robot. Pála grinned at me and at her Geordie gravedigger husband, who knew the words without even looking at the sheet. The song was a lot like Islands In The Stream but without ever getting to the "and we rely on each other, uh-hu-uh" bit. Leo began to sing Islands In The Stream, a chunk of pink light from outside sat on his hair. Cathy was just laughing, and the buttery little boy was licking the back of his hands. As the song finished, someone tapped on their wine glass with a fork, people clapped and stamped their feet and looked to Inga and Magnus. The couple climbed up onto their chairs and kissed, arms round necks and getting cheered along by their guests.

"They have to do that every time anyone taps a glass," Pála told me. "It's traditional." So as soon as Inga and Magnus sat down, I tapped my glass and they got up, laughing, back on their chairs, and kissed again. More cheering.

Once we'd eaten our kalkúnasalat and our plokkfiskur and sung more Icelandic songs and made the newlyweds kiss half a dozen times more, there was a speech from Inga's dad. He began quietly and shuffled about. As he went on he got chattier. The words sounded stretchy and soft and fond. Inga gazed at him, grinning. He made a joke about Magnus, I think, and Magnus laughed along with everyone else. Then he got a bit serious, his chin ducked down a little, he looked to his wife, Inga's mum, and said something that made everyone go, "Awww." Then he turned back to all of us, raised his glass and said, "Skál!"

"Skál!" we all said, or something like that. "Skál!"

Then Inga gave a speech. "First of all I'd like to mention," she said, climbing up onto her chair, "how wonderful I look." Then she said the same thing, I think, in Icelandic, and then she was talking – in Icelandic but with these slivers of English – about her parents, and Magnus, and her friends, and the food, and she toasted us all, "Skál!" And we toasted her, "Skál!", and we toasted her and Magnus, and her parents, and everyone there and all of our selves, "Skál! Skál! Skál! Skál!"

The band that played after we'd cleared away the tables and drunk more wine seemed to be the greatest wedding band imaginable, singing Come On Eileen and Crazy In Love in Icelandic, singing Ticket To Ride in English but actually screaming it more than singing it, almost at double speed, seething.

"My phone's died," Leo said. He was sitting by me, tired from doing his Beyoncé dance, trying to text his wife. He had shown me photos of his two children earlier, a newborn peachy thing and a little boy with bags under his eyes.

"You want to borrow mine?" My phone was in my coat pocket, under a table somewhere across the room. It would be weird though, I thought, for him to text from the phone of a woman his wife hardly knew.

"Fuck it," he said, and leant back. He was watching Inga and Magnus doing a kind of jive, with a circle of friends around them.

Cathy came and sat with us, rosy-cheeked from dancing. "Uh-oh, uh-oh, uh-oh!" she sang, and jiggled her shoulders.

"Sausage rolls!" Leo said, eyes lit up as he saw Inga's mum and auntie arranging plates of leftovers on a table in the corner.

"More coleslaw!" said Cathy. I thought it was about an hour since we'd eaten, two at the most, but the pair of them were straight over there, digging in.

I stood up once they'd left me on my own, and I walked, adrift, around the edge of the party. Inga's uncle, who looked like Leonard Cohen if Leonard Cohen was an elf, strolled up to me, gave a half-bow and offered a hand, swung me onto the dancefloor. He slid his hand round to the small of my back and chatted away to me as we danced. Maybe he didn't realise that I couldn't understand a word. It was nice to listen to the noises he made anyway and to dance with an old married man. I was clumsy and slow on my feet, and I pushed my hips towards him. Who was being nice to who? The band was singing, "You know that I could be in love with almost everyone, I think that people are the greatest fun," and I did what I considered to be some kind of cha-cha. Leonard Cohen smiled, chuckled even. I thought his wife might be watching, rankled. I wondered if I looked foolish. One strap fell off my shoulder. I watched his eyes taking aim at my breasts. Perhaps he could see where my nipples were through the silk. I must have fun, I decided, I will dance merrily through all the indignities. Nothing to be sad about here.

Magnus and Inga came over and intercepted us in the middle of a twirl. Inga grabbed her uncle and I got Magnus, they must have worked it out between them first. It felt much worse to be dancing with the groom.

"Hallo," he said.

"Hello."

"You okay?"

"Yes. What a beautiful day. Thanks for inviting me."

"Thanks for coming."

"This is a great party."

"Good band, huh?"

And on we went like that until the song finished and I went outside, where the sky was pinks and blues and a few people were smoking. A couple – English, and a little younger than me and Leo and Cathy – were describing the previous day, which they'd spent at the blue lagoon a few miles away. As he spoke, about the warm water and the jets of steam and the bar where you could buy a Blue Lagoon cocktail, her eyes darted from his face to all of our faces. The fingers on her right hand tapped and tickled the engagement ring on her left hand. He kept on talking. "We spent ages in the sauna bit," he said. "Drinking these cocktails."

"We were there quite early," his fiancee said, looking at him now. "There was hardly anyone around."

I looked to another man, a friend of Inga's or maybe a cousin, who was standing looking at this couple as if they were a deformed exhibit in the natural history museum.

"Hallo," I said, in a way that I thought might convey some sort of relaxed kinship and shared but not unkind distaste for certain other people, with just those two syllables and a lift of my eyebrows. He was chewing a little pad of tobacco. He was tall and he had soft, fine hair like a child's, and soft, smooth skin, although he was in his early forties, maybe, or late thirties. Another man, smaller and smilier, came and stood next to him, grinned at me, and the engaged couple walked away without saying anything.

"Some trolls over there, I think," the smaller man said.

"Oh yeah?" said the tobacco man, with a nod.

"Trolls!" I said, grabbing the word like a lifebuoy. "Trolls are big in Iceland, hey?"

"Trolls are small," said the tobacco man, giving me a babysitter smile.

"You believe in trolls though?"

"It's not whether we believe in them or not," he told me. "There they are."

"There they are," said the smaller man. "Look at the rocks. When you see the little rocks, there they are."

I looked over and saw, here and there across the grassy land, dark rocks in pairs and in threes.

"They're hidden in the rocks?" I said.

"Or they are the rocks," said the smaller man. "They turn into rocks if they're caught out by the sunlight."

"It must be shit to be a troll in summer in Iceland," I said.

Leo and Cathy were standing next to me now. Leo was smiling at the two men, a drunk man radiating non-alpha-male friendliness.

"You know what time it is?" he asked.

The tobacco man got a watch out of his pocket and gave it a stroke. "Broken," he said, regretfully.

About five yards away, out in front of the scout hut, a group of Icelandic guests had gathered in a great big circle, holding hands. The pink light made everyone look beautiful, unless it was the wine. They began to sing – the hokeycokey. I was laughing. The universal pastime of hokeycokey-ing. Leo and

Cathy had already joined in and I shimmied my way between the big Simon Callow man and a skinny, pretty man who might have been his boyfriend.

"In OOT! In OOT!" we sang, kicking back and forth with our right leg, our left leg, our whole selves. The rest of that bit I sang in English but with an urge to rhyme – "Shake it all ab-OOT" – and then I mumbled the rest. We gathered in, all together, and out again, in-in-in to a tight boozy circle and back out-out-out but still holding hands, the circle intact. After we'd put our whole selves in and our whole selves out, and shaken it all about in Icelandic, the group dispersed, people went to get drinks, light cigarettes.

"Let's go and commune with the trolls," Cathy said. She had her shoes off again and a bottle of wine in her hand. We headed towards the rocks and grass, towards the pink horizon where the sun seemed to be sliding along, peeking at us, giving no sense of the time. My phone was still in my bag under that table and neither of us wore a watch. Leo ran towards the light, arms out, making zooooooooom noises.

"Is it strange to be away from the kids?" I asked Cathy. She had two boys.

"No, not really, it's nice to have a break, stay up late, not worry about the babysitter. It'll be nice to see them when I get home."

I couldn't remember if Cathy's sister, also a good friend of mine, was pregnant again. Sometimes I thought I'd imagined pregnancies and births among my friends. I wasn't losing track though – it always turned out they actually were pregnant, or they actually had had another child. Or sometimes a miscarriage.

"Ouch!" Cathy had stepped on something sharp.

"Angry trolls," I said. "Watch it, we're trespassing."

She hopped up onto a bigger rock, a couple of feet tall, and stretched her arms out like an opera singer. She couldn't think of a song, though, and so she just opened her mouth and started laughing.

Leo was up ahead of us. "I want to take photos," he said. "To show the kids. Anyone got a camera? A phone?"

We didn't.

"You'll have to remember it and then render it in oil or perhaps watercolour for them," Cathy said, putting an arm through Leo's and smiling up at him all silly.

"Kate could do that," Leo said. His wife was an artist. "I'm better with a camera."

"They wouldn't be interested in pictures anyway," said Cathy. "Stop fooling yourself. They want sweets and a cuddly toy from the airport."

"A cuddly toy," said Leo. "That's what they'll have, a nice cuddly seal or a whale. A chunk of volcanic rock if they're lucky."

We were heading further and further away from the party, as if we might get to see the sun properly if we got far enough round the horizon, or as if we were actually looking for trolls. Then a little further up the hill we saw a bench. It looked incongruous in a place where you could imagine – if you were citydwellers like us – that no people ever came.

The bench seemed to be thoughtlessly positioned. Instead of looking out on the glorious Icelandic vista available a few yards further up the hill, it faced up the looming slope so that you got horizon and sky a little way above you. Next to it was an angled metal lectern with etched illustrations of native birds, all named in Icelandic.

"Toppskarfur," I said, in my Icelandic accent that brought out my latent Bolton accent mixed with the Swedish Chef. "What do you think that is? Topp-skar-fur. Fyll." I looked at another one. "*Fyll.* What would that be in England?" The birds did not look familiar, I couldn't identify anything.

Leo stood next to me, maybe looking at the lectern too. "Ah well, they don't know either," he said.

"Look at these two," I pointed at a couple of black-and-white seabirds strutting about a few yards away.

Leo pulled some tiny biscuits from his pocket, in cellophane wrappers. "From the plane," he said. I took a couple and we crumbled them, threw them to the birds.

"Are you a toppskarfur?" I asked one as it approached.

"He doesn't look toppskarfic," said Leo, throwing more biscuits. No other birds came, it was just these two.

Cathy was looking in the direction of the scout hut. "We should get back to the reception. I want some more of that coleslaw."

"I'll stay here a bit I think. I fancy a sit-down." I smiled and they smiled, and they strolled off towards the singing and dancing.

I watched them for a minute then I stood up on the bench, walked along it, steady enough on my high heels, looking down at my feet and feeling the sky around me. Things happen, one after another, whether we believe it or not. I stopped and looked around, saw birds – toppskarfurs, perhaps, or fylls – soaring, flapping, strutting. Then I jumped off the end of the bench, walked back to the middle, sat there for a while and watched the sun coming up (or going down).

Chronicle of a
Baffled Spinster

MAY

The whole day before their date she is extremely careful crossing roads and feels nervous when the tube stops in a tunnel. She just wants one date with this man. It would be awful if she was knocked over or killed before they'd even had their first date.

Tony has dark ginger hair, honey-freckled skin, brown eyes and a broken nose. She thinks he is the kind of beautiful that only she finds beautiful, so that (a) there won't be too much competition and (b) he will be grateful for her attentions. It turns out she is wrong about both these things.

They sit in the park, his jacket laid out on the grass, drinking champagne from the bottle. He sings "I wanna hold your hand", and holds her hand. Later when he kisses her he whispers, "I like you." She wishes she could get that in writing. The next day he sends a text message that just says "xxx". She worries about what to text back.

On what she thinks is their second date, in a pub with some of Tony's friends, he tells her he met the woman he's going to marry last week. After a dizzy second she realises he isn't talking about her. She spends the next half hour listening to Tony's friend Richard, who explains that he never gets involved with women who don't trim their pubic hair properly. "A messy bush is a sign of low self-esteem," he says.

Tony walks her to the taxi rank. "You're a fox," he says. "You're a superfox. I'm really sorry." But he's happy to have met someone, all jittery and smiles about this girl. "We own all the same records," he says, astonished.

She tells the taxi driver that the man she likes is in love with someone else. "Well, that's a kick in the teeth," he tells her. At home, she gets halfway up the stairs before she sits down to cry.

JUNE

One Tuesday morning, riding her bicycle down Clements Hill, she closes her eyes for five full seconds, her mind held quiet, waiting.

JULY

She and Stella both blag the afternoon off work and meet at the park. The sun is full out and baking, and they lie in the heat with nothing to do. They get Orange Maid lollies from an ice-cream van. They stroke and pull on the long grass, watch ladybirds and spiders, follow birds across the sky.

The sunlight dazzles in Stella's shiny hair, as if the two were made for playing together. The noise of other people is a cosy distant wall around their calm and quiet spot. They take off their shoes and lie on their bellies, toes wriggling against the earth and cheeks collapsed on arms, eyes squinting in the sun.

AUGUST

She watches eight episodes of The Wire in one Saturday and slowly eats three silver trays of takeaway curry. She's so happy she could cry.

SEPTEMBER

At Chloe's house party, she wears a slinky dress and feels sexy.

"This guy Jack just asked about you," Chloe tells her. "You'll like him. He's cute."

Jack is in the lounge talking to Chloe's boyfriend Mike. They are looking at the back of a Funkadelic CD. They tell each other that George Clinton is really fucking cool.

She and Chloe walk over. She puts Bonnie Tyler on the stereo – Total Eclipse Of The Heart. It's a karaoke classic, although there's no chance of karaoke here. Chloe starts talking quietly to Mike, stroking his arm. He has one finger hooked in the front of her top.

Bonnie sings. *We're living in a powder keg and giving off sparks.*

Jack smiles, already pleased with himself, then opens his mouth to say something to her.

"Why do women wear make-up and perfume?" she asks him.

"I don't know." He frowns. "Why *do* women wear make-up and perfume?"

"Because they're ugly and they smell."

"Oh," says Jack. He turns to change the CD.

OCTOBER

In the pub one Friday after work she is trapped in a discussion about the rights of terror suspects. Mark, a friend of Karen's, is mispronouncing habeas corpus. *Habby*-uss corpus. When he makes a point he's especially pleased with he says, "Think about it," afterwards, and raises his eyebrows at her.

"The world is a dangerous and complicated place," he tells her. He uses her name when he talks to her. She is laughing, at him. His eyes have stopped flicking back and forth between her face and her breasts. She imagines holding the back of his head by the hair, smashing his face into her knee.

NOVEMBER

One lunchtime, hungover, she goes to the small pharmacy near her office to get the morning-after pill. As the chemist is explaining possible side-effects, her mouth starts to water and the blood plummets out of her head. The chemist catches her and helps her to a chair, gives her glucose tablets and talks softly about blood sugar. The woman behind the counter fetches a plastic cup of water.

The next day, she takes a box of Roses chocolates to the pharmacy. "Thank you," she smiles, leaving it on the counter. "For yesterday, thanks."

DECEMBER

"Have fun while you're still young," her grandma tells her. "It's no fun being old."

"You were always harder than your sister," Auntie Kim says. "She's easier. You set very high standards."

JANUARY

Chloe phones. "Mike's leaving me," she says, matter-of-fact. "He says he hasn't really been happy for two or three years." They've been together for four years.

FEBRUARY

"You've got a lovely ledge," Dr Flinson tells her, two latex-gloved fingers curled into her. This doctor always runs warm water over the speculum before she does a smear, and is gentle and fast on internal exams. This is the nicest clinic in town, all her friends are scraped and poked and reassured here. (Although Karen had her abortion here a few years ago and during the scan the nurse turned the screen round to point out the "baby".)

MARCH

One morning, sitting on the toilet, she notices a pubic hair – an outpost, a traitor – sprouted on her inside thigh just a couple of inches above her knee.

APRIL

She goes to a gig on her own. The band is loud and fast. She walks home, looking around her, thinking "moon-oiled rooftops" and singing "star light, star bright, the star I see tonight." At home in bed the sheets are smooth, they brush soft against her ear.

Wild Nights!

Behind the decks, but not DJing, stood a blonde woman who was familiar to me. I had seen her before, maybe lots of times, at other parties. She stood surveying the room like she was a bouncer for the DJ, leaning back with her chin out, not dancing but moving ever so slightly to the music.

I'd put my coat on at least twenty minutes ago but then I'd been pulled back by an amazing Fern Kinney song and I was still there, partly because James had given me another cup of MDMA punch and partly because the music was solid joy. And partly because of the blonde, who didn't seem to have noticed me yet.

It was a small-ish house party. The floor was wooden, wet with drink, records splayed in collapsed piles around the sides of where we were dancing. Oliver was on his hands and knees, pushing the records back out of the way, trying to keep them safe, like a man with a broom trying to brush back flood waters. I was saying to James, "If I had a cock I'd fuck you with it," earnest and ravenous at the thought. He laughed and hugged me, snuggled my neck. James's friend Grace hugged him. It was her birthday party but she was subdued, floating about and cuddling her guests. We all sat down on the sofa. James took a biro out of his back pocket, and started to draw a pretend tattoo on my forearm. It felt tickly and good.

"What's her name?" I asked him, nodding to the blonde. She was about eight feet away, but the music was loud enough that she wouldn't hear.

"Gloria," he said, and spelled it out like Patti Smith: "G-L-O-R-I-I-I-I-I-I... G-L-O-R-I-A."

Gloria looked over. Right then Paulie stopped the music dead for a second, and then he played Gene Vincent. Be-Bop-A-Lula. Gloria moved in front of the decks. She was small and she had on a pair of jeans, bare feet with pearly toenails, a pale blue vest, no bra. Skinny and small, but not like a little girl. Like a boilwashed woman. Hard all over, like a rich boilwashed woman who does a lot of yoga. She danced to Gene Vincent. Outside the sun was thinking about coming up. I watched Gloria. She danced with her eyes open but not looking anywhere. She would bend around, lean back, swing forward, slow slow slow, her arms up but all loose, her wrists floppy. She danced like she was dodging bullets in The Matrix. Sometimes she would lift a leg, bend it at the knee maybe, put her bare foot back down on the sticky floor.

I looked down and James had written YES YES MORE MORE on my arm, in big wobbly letters. The song finished and Gloria sat down right next to me on the sofa and kissed me. It was a fairly unobtrusive hello kiss which turned into something with tongues and a hand on my leg. I don't know if we talked first or not. I remember her checking at some point that I wasn't with James. "You're not going home with him are you?" is what she said. "Oh, no!" I said, as if I wouldn't dream of going home with a beautiful, interesting, funny, kind man. James was busy now anyway, he was standing in the corner playing air piano. I leaned forward and kissed Gloria again, as if to seal my point.

There was a taxi coming just as we got outside so I flagged it down and opened the door for Gloria, waved her in like I had an imaginary hat in my hand with feathers in it. "Why, thank you, how kind," she said, and climbed in. You can be quite elegant climbing into a black cab, it turns out, when you are small and bouncy on your feet.

She gave the driver her address and I held the cup of punch I'd brought from the party at arm's length because it was slopping about a bit as we turned corners. Gloria had slipped her shoes off again and was doing tiny Mexican waves with her toes, then she swung to face me and slid a foot up the front of my leg, like a flirty dinner date. About five seconds later the taxi stopped because we were outside her house. We could have walked there in two minutes.

And inside, there we were inside her flat. Wild Nights! I thought. Wild Nights! I couldn't remember the rest of the poem though. Emily Dickinson. There's a line about waves, maybe, there is desire and there's a port, somewhere to stay for the night.

Gloria took me straight to bed. She was softer than she looked. Her body was a warm, exciting echo of mine. She tasted good. She smelled good. She felt good. It was new to me.

"Wake up," she whispered in the morning. Or the afternoon by then. "I made you tea. I put sugar in it. Two sugars. And do you want some toast?" She was stroking my hair. She had just her blue vest on and she got up, walked across the bedroom and through the hall to the main room, with the sofa and the kitchen and the stereo and the bookshelves and the telly. Her bottom was whiter than the rest of her, where a bikini had been. When I walked through she was standing by the toaster. I liked looking at her while she made my breakfast.

"Marmalade," I said, because I could see the marmalade. And then I saw the butter and said, "Mmm, butter." I had a hangover.

She glanced round at me and then got back to my breakfast. Her tits were smaller than mine and her belly was bigger. She was lovely. She was singing along to I've Had The Time Of

My Life – Gloria in fact owned the Dirty Dancing soundtrack on vinyl and there it was, spinning around on top of a low bookshelf.

The second song on that album is The Ronettes' Be My Baby, and Gloria sang along to that too, hips banging to one side at the "cha" of the "dum du-dum cha" drum beat. Twenty minutes later we'd eaten toast and drunk tea and we were dancing to Yes, which is the last song on side one, sung by Merry Clayton.

"This is the woman who did the backing vocals on Gimme Shelter," I told Gloria, who didn't care or didn't hear me. She had turned up the volume and was scissoring her arms up in the air and doing the twist. She was the opposite of the blonde woman swaying behind the decks last night. We danced together and sometimes we bounced on the sofa, close to falling over. She still had no knickers on, and no bra so her little tits were bouncing under her blue vest. The song was brilliant, I wondered how I'd never noticed it before.

It was sunny and still only the middle of the afternoon. Gloria lent me a summer dress which was too tight on me and we went to Regent's Park, ten minutes' walk from her flat. We didn't see anyone I knew, but two friends of hers were walking up the main path towards us with their dog. "Ooh," she said. "It's Brett and Heather." They smiled and stopped and talked and Gloria introduced me. I didn't say a word, I just smiled at them like some mute mysterious girl, leaning towards Gloria so I could smell her all the time. Gloria's fingers were going up and down my backbone as if she was playing slow scales on a sideways piano.

Brett and Heather had just been out on the boating lake and we decided we'd do that too. Gloria got us ice-creams and I got the tickets. We climbed in and I lay back while she rowed us into the middle.

"You comfy?" she asked, looking at me with her DJ bouncer expression again. I was holding onto the side of the boat with one hand and trying to eat my 99 without dripping ice-cream everywhere. I was holding her ice-cream too, in the same hand, and the boat was swaying a bit too much. Gloria paddled us away from the other people on the lake, into a shady, darker part of the water.

"You're strong for a little thing." I sounded like a dirty old man.

"How do you know Grace?" she asked. It took me a few seconds to remember that it was Grace's party we were at last night.

"She works with my good friend Stella. Do you know Stella?"

"I think she works with Dougie, my ex-boyfriend."

"Oh, at the new Kingsland Road place?" I didn't care about any of this.

"Yeah, exactly. I met her at their Christmas party last year."

She was watching me as she talked. There is no way to know what someone is thinking when they look at you.

We were by the wooded island in the middle of the lake, near the moorhens and their nests. Gloria pulled the oars into the boat. A distant panic niggled me, that trawling hangover anxiety. I kept quiet and watched while she ate her ice-cream and told me about her work. She was a lawyer, working with musicians. Or maybe an accountant. While she talked she put her legs out, one foot on each side of me.

We floated away from the moorhens and I rowed us back over there, into the shade and the quiet.

"You're lovely," she said.

I leaned to one side, looked up through the hole in a polo-mint cloud, felt suspicions of unconsidered possibilities.

I didn't want to go home that night so I didn't go home. I stayed at Gloria's flat. I used her toothbrush again and wore her silky nightie. The next day was Monday so we'd have to get up for work, both of us. We sat on the sofa, got a curry delivered and watched most of Antiques Roadshow.

That night when she was giving me head I realised it was the best head I'd ever had in my life and I laughed a bit, thinking, Oh what a cliche that women really do know how to do it better, how funny if that's true. And most men would have stopped, if I was laughing while they were giving me head, but Gloria didn't stop, she grabbed the tops of my legs, there was maybe a giggle, she knew what was happening, and there was nothing wrong, it was all right.

In the morning I got up first and had a wash, my biro tattoo almost gone, then made Gloria a cup of tea while she had her shower. She listened to the news on the radio. She dried her hair. I watched her get dressed – a white blouse, see-through with a slip underneath, and a black pencil skirt. "Keys, money, phone," she said, and gave a quick bright smile. "Ready." Outside, on the pavement, she kissed me and slinked off to the tube in her heels with her hair piled up, like someone playing at being a sexy secretary. I headed towards the bus stop in my Saturday night clothes, knickers not even inside out. No one can tell, I thought, and they wouldn't care anyway.

Over the road there was a school, with a group of girls around eight years old playing in the yard outside. I hadn't seen children playing in a playground since I was at school myself and the scene looked to me like something from the 1980s. I slowed down and walked diagonally across the street so I could watch them a while without stopping to stare. There were six girls. Two of them turned a skipping rope while another jumped the rope. Two other girls faced one another, alongside the rope, and played a clap-hands game. The girls were all singing and these two clapped along in time to the song while the jumping girl jumped in time. Another girl stood waiting, watching the others, and she was singing too, with her hands on her hips.

They weren't singing a traditional skipping song, whatever that would be, they were singing that Adele song: "There's a fire, starting in my heart." Their quiet, straightforward voices plucked each syllable, turning fire into 'fii-yer' to fit the extra beat. At the end of one line, or on some signal that I didn't catch, one of the clapping girls moved into the rope, began to skip, and the skipping girl moved around to where the waiting girl had been, and the waiting girl began to clap with the remaining clapping girl.

They didn't miss a beat or a word. I couldn't make sense of what was happening in the few seconds that I saw them, but they all knew how the game worked and they were absorbed in it. Other children were playing and yelling and running, or chatting in small groups and waiting for classes to start, but these six girls didn't see them. Perhaps I could have stopped to watch and they wouldn't have noticed me either. Together they had a mechanical elegance. At some point one of them was bound to get it wrong. "Rolling in the deep," they sang, clapped, skipped. "Rolling in the deep." I kept walking.

Sorrow, Borrow

"Baby, baby, where did our love go?"

The radio's on and I'm singing along while I wash up, the bubbles soft against my skin. It's a sunny day.

"Don't you want me, don't you want me no more?"

Glass, hot water, wipe, rinse, draining board.

"I've got this yearning burning yearning feeling inside me."

And a spin and a handclap before the mug, which I swirl in the hot dirty water, baby baby, ooh baby baby, and rinse, and I slide along the kitchen floor to that trombone (is it a trombone?) and stamp my feet and swing my hips and then I just get on with it – cutlery – and keep singing. The doorbell rings as the song's finishing, and I'm glad it's finished because I know who's at the door.

What I wasn't expecting though was that she'd have the baby with her. He's got lots of dark curly hair already, he's always looking around, and he's giggly. Kelly has him wrapped in a white blanket. She leaves the pram in the hallway and carries him so he's looking over her shoulder, so when she walks ahead he's looking at me. She goes straight into the front room and lays him down in the middle of the rug, his legs are bare and so are his feet. He kicks about for a minute then stops, suddenly entranced by the ceiling, by the light fitting maybe which is silver and fancy with frosted bulbs behind thick glass. He freezes, mouth open, cute. The light fitting is something Kelly chose, I expect. I would have just got one of those paper lanterns.

I lived on my own for years and then I moved in with my lover, into the place he'd shared with his old lover. He left her after he fell in love with me, except he didn't leave – he stayed in the flat and she moved out, with their boy, and I moved in. I didn't sell my place, mind.

And now she is here to collect some things, as arranged with Frank earlier in the week. He's not here because he has gone to play football in the park with his friends like he does most Saturdays in the summer. He won't be back for a couple of hours, which is why Kelly has come over now. But we didn't want her in the flat on her own, or I didn't anyway, so here I am.

I turn the radio off and put the kettle on. She hasn't said anything yet. She's watching me open her old cupboard and get two mugs and go to the drawer for a teaspoon. We have never had a conversation, beyond a few words exchanged in the past maybe when we were sitting round the same table in a pub or standing at the same bar after a gig. She hardly ever came out with the rest of the people from work, even before she got pregnant, so it was easy to pretend that Frank was single. He rarely talked about her once the initial excitement of having a new girlfriend wore off, and that was three or four years ago.

"Shall I get something for Little Frank?" I ask her. She called the baby Frank which is, obviously, insane.

"No, he just had a feed."

"Do you want sugar?"

"No thanks."

She's sitting at the kitchen table and Little Frank is still in the other room.

"How's Frank?" she asks.

I launch into chatter. "He's had trouble at work all month because the new boss is reorganising everything and more to the point she just doesn't seem to like him very much. He's talking about leaving soon but I don't think he will. I think the new boss will leave, actually, it looks to me like she's only been brought in to shake things up and show that the old era is over and the lean, mean times have arrived. That's how it usually works, isn't it? Then she'll be whisked away to another division to freak someone else out with her shark eyes and her I'm-your-friend-but-if-you-do-not-agree-with-me-I-will-destroy-you vibe. Oh god, you don't know her do you?"

"Not really," says Kelly. Then she smiles, which feels like I've been given a small, delicate prize. I plunge onwards.

"I had a few meetings with her years ago when we were redesigning. I was young and I didn't know how to spot a sociopath. Made the mistake of assuming she was an actual human being. She's fucking not. She asked me to meet her for a coffee one morning, for a 'chat', and it was an ambush. She started off about friends, boyfriends, where I grew up, then we talk about work and she starts taking notes. Which is weird, no?"

Kelly nods. She looks to the other room – Little Frank is gurgling.

"Shall we check on him?" I ask her and then I walk to the hall, have a look at the baby.

"What's he doing?" she calls through.

"He's still looking at the ceiling. He seems happy enough. Does his nappy need changing or anything?" I kneel beside him, put my face close to his, smile, say, "Hello Frankie," tickle his belly. He smiles, laughs, and his left hand reaches up, knocks into my cheek. He is brilliant. I take hold of his ankle and blow a raspberry on the sole of his foot. This seems to be the funniest thing that's ever happened to Little Frank, he explodes in wriggles and giggles. I wonder what Kelly is doing and get back into the kitchen. She is looking in the fridge.

"Are you hungry?" I say, and she turns round slowly, her face tilted down. She shuts the fridge door and leans back against the counter.

"Do you want him, Annie?" she says. "He sleeps pretty well. He doesn't cry much." She smiles at me again and does a strange blinking and staring thing, sucks in her lips. Then she walks past me into the hall and through to the spare room, which is where we've put all her stuff, anything she didn't take with her to her mum's. It's just a few boxes and some bin bags.

"I'll give you a hand."

"You keep an eye on Little Frank," she tells me. She's taller than me and staggers past with a box that would knock straight into my face if she just staggered a bit to the left. She stops at the door and looks at me, waits, and I lean over to let her out. I leave the door on the latch and watch her go slowly down the stairs, leaning backwards like she's heavily pregnant but at chest height. When she gets back upstairs I'm on the living room floor again, leaning against the sofa, looking at Little Frank. He isn't doing much.

Kelly's tied her hair back. She takes the second box, and the third, then the last one, then the big John Lewis bag with some material she'd bought to have curtains made.

"I don't want to go just yet," she says. She's in the kitchen now, Little Frank is still in the front room.

"Frank won't be home for a while," I say. Does she want to see him?

"Good."

"Have another drink."

She's looking at her hands.

"Is it too early to have wine?" I say, walking over to the bottle standing on the side. Red. "Are you still breastfeeding?"

"Just one," she says, and smiles. "I'm driving, and breastfeeding, so I shouldn't really."

I pour two, put them on the table. She's looking at the draining board, at Frank's mug that he got on holiday in Crete once, upside down where I left it to dry. My phone gives a buzz – text message – which I ignore and she doesn't.

"Is he waiting for the all-clear?" she asks, looking at the phone on the kitchen counter instead of looking at me.

"He'll still be playing," I say. "Or in the pub, maybe."

She goes to get Little Frank from the front room and I think, How can I stop this happening? And then she walks back in, sits back down, sits Little Frank up on her lap, takes her glass of wine with her spare hand. I sit down and look at her across the table, and at Little Frank who has brown eyes and a dimpled chin.

"We need a thingy to sit him in," I say. Turns out we have one – Kelly directs me out to the hall and after a bit of faffing I take the top part off the pram and it's a little seat that holds up soft-spined babies while the grown-ups drink merlot. Little Frank sits like a half-deflated balloon, sometimes he's watching us and his arms will both float up into the air and he'll smile. Or his mouth will fall open a bit and he'll put something in it – Kelly has given him a little plastic truck to chomp on, but other times it's just his hand.

"So work's the same as ever, is it?" she asks.

"Yeah. You thinking of going back to your place anytime soon?" Kelly used to work at a recruitment company.

"I'm still doing some bits and pieces for them, from home. I'm not sure it's worth it though."

Frank is giving her money, for the baby.

"I'm on a retainer but it's only tiny," she goes on. "If it was any more it would start fucking up my maternity pay."

"Oh, right."

"But it's nice to keep your hand in. Nice to be getting the emails."

"You want to play with the grown-ups as well as the baby."

"Yeah. He's lovely though. He's really lovely."

"He does seem pretty brilliant." I look at Little Frank, who is looking at Kelly. "You're pretty brilliant, aren't you?" I say, in a high, exhaling voice.

He ignores me. Kelly gets up and goes into the bathroom, closes the door behind her. I look around the kitchen and then I look at the patch of carpet outside the bathroom. There's no sound from in there. I realise how quiet Little Frank is. He hasn't gurgled for a while. I can't even hear his breathing. I give him a little prod, and he giggles.

"You are a very happy young man." And I kiss the top of his soft hairy head, put my little finger inside his little fist to get that nice baby grip that they do. I shake his hand about a bit and touch my nose to his, which makes him giggle again.

No sound from the bathroom, unless that's the cabinet door closing. I sit back down and have just a little sip of wine. I text Frank back, tell him not to come home. Not yet, I mean. Little Frank is quiet again. He is the quietest baby I've ever met. There's not a sound in the flat, I try to hear the boiler even, nothing. A bit of traffic outside.

Then the toilet flushes and I feel ashamed that I've been listening so carefully. She comes back out and sits down.

"Do you want some more wine?" I say. I get up to fetch the bottle from the counter so I can pour her another inch or two.

And now the baby's crying, a soft and empty cry. We both look at him, tired, and his cry gets louder and more purple-faced. Kelly reaches over to rub the top of his back, between his small shoulders. "It's okay, darling," she says. "It's okay." I pause, at the counter, and I think Kelly's about to cry too but she doesn't. She looks at me and starts to laugh, her head tilts back but she's looking at me, her chest and belly shaking. Who won, is what I'm thinking. Who won here, and when is it time to leave? Then I sit back down and laugh right along with her.

Sex in New Orleans

Annie Marshall set out alone from her north London flat on a sunshiney summer afternoon for a good long walk. She'd been bored and irritated all day, working at home, so she headed out into the pink light with the hope that fresh air and a stroll might calm her muddled brain.

It was July, and after a few half-hearted weeks something like summer had set in. Edward Square was muggy and full of people and prams and dogs. Towards King's Cross, where she headed down Copenhagen Street and past the car wash, Annie looked around and saw almost no one down the hill and across the canal and by the wide open steps along its edge, just a woman walking a small terrier and a car or two droning by. The sun began to sink as she walked across and towards Camden, alongside the water, running through her day's work, trying to knock it into shape. An hour passed and, realising that the walk wasn't doing much for her sleepy anxiety, Annie headed up the next main road and sat at the bus stop by the small cemetery there. The 274 bus would drop her back at home.

It felt odd; there was no one else at the bus stop or anywhere in sight. A few cars went along the tree-lined road by the cemetery but that was all. There was no one in the flower shop, not even a florist, and no one in the stonemason's yard, where crosses and headstones leaned up against the wall. It was cloudy now. Annie looked at the honeysuckle covering the pretty blue-tiled crematorium, let her mind follow the petals' curves and the twisting stalks, thought about work, thought about her meeting tomorrow, even came up with some half-formed feature ideas.

A few minutes later she was still sitting there, with buses quite likely gone past, when she noticed a figure in the porch of the brick office a few feet beyond the crematorium. He was standing and peering out as if he was hiding from the rain, even though there wasn't any.

She wasn't sure whether he'd come out of the office or the crematorium, or from the street or the cemetery. Not too tall, thin, clean-shaven, with a stubby fat nose, he had copper hair and a milky, freckled face. He looked alien, otherworldly. He did, though, have a grey canvas bag hanging from one shoulder, wore a pair of jeans and muddy trainers. Though he wasn't old, he had a walking stick which he held with both hands on top, the cane leaning diagonally from the ground, with one of his ankles crossed over the other. He looked like he might topple over as he looked up.

Annie had been watching the man sleepily and perhaps not discreetly, and she was knocked awake when she realised he was staring right back at her. She shifted on the bench and turned away, as if to check up the road for that bus, and decided she wouldn't take any more notice of this strange character.

A moment later she'd forgotten him, distracted by something else: there was a sudden expansion in her chest, a dizzy lurch and soar, and a panicky urge for lost adventure. Annie was scared to move, and her hands held tight to the front edge of the bench. Then her brain filled with pictures of warm pavements and sticky cocktails, strange smiles and new hands to hold. She saw a sultry city, a glooping and glittering world of blossoming trees and pearls. She saw long fingers tapping songs on a tabletop, one leg crossed louche across the other, a fresh drink coming over. She saw water flowing slowly, green and topped with wet dust, cawing birds ignoring her, beautiful and jerky, clumsily flying. Then the dream left her, and with a sniff Annie leaned back on the bench, one ankle pulled up now onto the other knee, and breathed in slow and deep.

She took two weeks' holiday every year, plus that week between Christmas and new year, and she had a few weekends away. She was an editor, for magazines and occasionally working on books too. She'd got quite serious about herself really, as a fixture in a far-reaching and fairly well-to-do professional network. She'd been in love, though not for some time. She even lived with a man for a while, but that turned out to be no good at all. Still, she thought she'd probably stay in London forever, in her nice little flat, and keep on skipping to Spain or Italy every summer.

The idea of disappearing to a place of sunshine and sticky drinks and glinting eyes was vague and silly. Then Annie thought about work, and those hours of staring blankly at a screen that stares blankly back. She was good at her job, but she had started to feel disdainful of those who praised her work and asked for more. She thought about the next few months, in her flat working or sometimes at the office, or out late in bars with friends and colleagues. A few years ago she used to walk home at two in the morning, barefoot and drunk, contentedly half-lost along orangey streets, but these days she muttered and wished grumpily for a taxi.

She wanted an adventure – how cheesy – and she had the money to do it. Savings, a few, and she could rent out the flat. So she would go away, maybe a long way away, to the tigers. A night on a plane under a thin blanket. A month or two, or three, somewhere friendly and warm.

And like that it was decided, as the bus approached between parked cars and slowed up for her. She was already impatient to look at airfares and hotels and weather forecasts. She thought, too, to glance back at the man with the stubby nose, her companion during that invisibly dramatic wait at the bus stop, but she couldn't see him. He wasn't under the porch anymore, or in the cemetery, or on the street, and he didn't follow her onto the bus.

*

A fortnight later Annie had organised for her friend Joe to stay in her flat and cover some of the mortgage. She'd done it before, when she moved in with her ex. Joe would rent out the spare room and that money would go straight into Annie's current account. It would be tight but doable. She told friends and colleagues that she was taking a sabbatical for a couple of months, maybe more. Then she set off for Perpignan, on the Eurostar from St Pancras and then from Paris straight down the middle of France.

She wanted somewhere warm and abroad, but somewhere easy, so she was heading to the holiday house of her aunt Pauline, which she could borrow anytime it was empty. The house was five minutes' walk from the seafront, a little way outside Perpignan on a small square surrounded by tall faded houses. She would sit there and drink Ricard and smile at the locals, wink at the old men.

She got there, though, and the locals didn't smile, the sun was hidden behind damp clouds, and she realised she had not found her final spot. On that first evening, sitting alone in the house, Annie's brain skipped around the world trying to imagine where she might feel right. A place where it wouldn't matter that she only spoke English. A place that was warm. A place with music and dancing. And not some place full of travellers finding themselves.

She realised – it was clear and fantastic – the perfect, dreamy spot. She packed up again and booked her flights, reserved a room in a sweet little guesthouse she found online. It took less than two hours. She would go straight there, not go back home. The next day she was on a train to Paris, and that evening she'd be on a flight across the Atlantic to Detroit, where she would take a connecting flight to her proper destination: New Orleans.

At Charles De Gaulle, dragging her bags, she saw a vast glass cave above her, enjoyed the noisy tiles under her feet. At check-in – passport in hand, passport on counter, hand luggage on shoulder, big bag on the conveyor belt – the groomed young man checked her photo and her visa, checked her face, and gazed softly at the screen while he typed. His hair was trimmed into straight lines behind his ears and across the back of his neck. His posture was straight like an obedient child's and his voice was even and smiling.

"Your bags will go straight through to New Orleans," he said, closing the passport and sliding it back over, rather slowly and wistfully, not looking up. "What a place! What a place. Amazing." He was almost mumbling. "Such a wonderful warm city! With the music, of course, and the food!" There was something strange happening, as if Annie wasn't going to New Orleans at all, as if it was this check-in man who was going and she had disappeared from the whole scenario. She took her passport, nodded and said, "Thank you. I'm very excited," but in a voice that was flat, and walked away, towards security and the departure lounge.

With one hand on the railing, leaning a little, she watched the people in front of her in the queue, waiting for the scanners and conveyor belts. A woman kept an eye on three small girls, one of whom was beaming and giggling at a security guard. A couple of teenagers leaned on the railing too, tapping their passports together and humming a song between them. And right in front of Annie a group of women in their thirties were chatting and laughing, all nudges and shrieks, prods and hilarity as they compared passport photos and pulled silly faces. One of them, wearing a yellow dress with a silky crimson scarf and big sparkly earrings, was somehow the centre of the action – taller, maybe, or louder. When Annie took a good look at her, though, she realised with a cringing delight that the woman was not like the others. She was old, simple as that; she had wrinkles down her cleavage and liver spots on her arms; her hair was dyed, badly; the skin on her neck was loose; her hands were claws, and her mouth was a bit too thin, her teeth a bit too yellow. What did her companions think, what did they say, about this old woman wearing their outfits, as if she was in her smooth, firm prime of life? They seemed to treat her like one of the gang, as an equal, laughing, touching her bare arms, with no quick glances to each other behind her old back. Annie put both hands on the railing, felt hot. Something was not quite right, it occurred to her, and she closed her eyes tight-tighter, hoping to reset her brain. She tried it again two minutes later and half-believed that the scanner, as she passed through it, might show something strange living inside her.

In seat 24H, with her bag in the locker above, Annie folded up her coat against the window so she could snuggle there. She watched the other passengers file in, shoving bags into gaps while air stewards went to and fro. The seat next to her was empty and she was pleased when it stayed that way. The dreaminess was starting to feel normal now. She didn't close her eyes tight to try to shake it away this time, she just took a slow breath and watched the people around her settle into their seats. She watched the safety video, and glimpsed the air steward who was strapped into her own little seat a few rows ahead. Annie felt her fingers tingle as the plane rolled along the runway and finally let her eyes fall closed. Just then, the plane revved and sped, she felt a floating sensation and, looking out the window almost in panic, saw the concrete below tilt and recede. After some wobbling and lurching they were up in the sky, heading higher and away. She must have been doing something odd because the steward, before the seatbelt sign was turned off, came over to see if she needed anything. Annie smiled, said no, I'm fine, thank you.

The air was clouds with stripes of light. There was no hint anymore of the land below. The wings shook and shuddered. With a blanket on her knees and another tucked around her shoulders, Annie watched through the small window and the hours passed. Dinner came and she left it in front of the seat beside her. They were in the pale blue, above the clouds. Below was land, or sea. In empty spaces and irrelevant scale, she thought, we float into the immeasurable. Smiling, chattering faces – the man with the copper hair, the woman with the wrinkled cleavage – seemed close by and familiar, and she fell asleep in their company.

Hours later she was given orange juice, a small soggy cake and slices of apple for breakfast. There was a low sun outside. Other passengers were stirring too, sleepy and compliant, their shoes lost under seats, children lying sideways with heads and feet on laps. The breakfast was foul but Annie finished it, thought it best to eat something, and then got back to the window, watching the sky. Detroit was beneath them, and her connection was smooth. It seemed inevitable, it felt reassuring, when the chatting, laughing women took the same onward flight as her. On the next plane they were just a few rows ahead, tired but still piled up with colour and accessories.

Sitting there, Annie imagined how it would be to arrive in New Orleans by ship instead, on a cruising steamboat, grand and stately. The air would be as wet as the river, her skin damp and warm too. The air in the plane was dry, and it was a little cold. She looked out over the wing and thought of the city waiting for her, the skinny balconies and the front steps, the shop windows to look in, the bars to drink in, the musicians playing old songs. Her chest felt light and tight, and her cheeks had lifted because her smile was so big.

Then beneath her were building and cars, people even, on the roads. The reveries became the beginnings of New Orleans. The seatbelt signs pipped on and the plane dipped gently down, until it touched the ground and the brakes rumbled and she felt like she'd landed from one dream into another.

It was some time before the passengers could get off the plane. The aircraft taxied about; it had arrived and it hadn't. The women from the airport were out of their seats and taking their bags from the lockers, finishing mini cans of coke. The older woman had black make-up all around her eyes and it was a bit depressing, really, to see her addled by the vodka they'd been drinking with the coke. She was all dehydrated and with sandpaper eyelids, no doubt, and a woolly tongue, and a savoury smell under her perfume. With her cigarettes and lighter in her hand already, she leaned back against one of the seats and eyed a man in his fifties with close-cropped hair and a solid bulk inside his white T-shirt. She licked her lips as she watched him, which made Annie smile. The feeling returned, the idea that the world was moving into a soft and foggy place, tilting. Then the doors opened and the passengers filed out, and the stewards said "thank you" and "goodbye" and "have a great time", which she planned to.

The sunshine air made her giggle and her eyes tingled as if she might cry. Inside the airport even the toilets felt like fun, too big and plasticky like part of a giant playhouse, and the queue for passport control was quick, and the luggage carousel seemed like it might play a song or deliver presents. When Annie's bag emerged she pulled it past the women, who were still waiting, a few sitting on bags that had arrived. The older woman held onto the back of a trolley, blinking softly at the rubber-fringed little hatch where the cases came out. She noticed when Annie passed by and leaned back, turned her head a little.

"Goodbye, honey," she said, in some grope at a Southern accent. "Enjoy yourself, enjoy yourself, see you around." And she smiled, almost a laugh, a little shudder of the chest. Then she kept talking, but not really to Annie anymore, saying, "Have fun, have some fun, take it easy in the Easy."

Annie felt a relief to be round the corner and out of her sight. A line of taxis waited, white and blue, to carry her into town. She headed straight to the front, there was no one else waiting, and the huge handsome driver got out to help with her bags.

"Welcome to New Orleans," he said, and his drawl was delicious.

Annie got into the back seat, which was lower down than she was expecting, and slippery. It was warm in the car and it smelled like cleaning product. The driver slid in, the back of his neck all damp, didn't look back at her and glided them straight out into the traffic.

"Louisa Street," said Annie. "Just between Burgundy and North Rampart." She said Bur-GUN-dy, felt self-conscious but liked it.

"Sure."

"Thanks."

Annie settled back, didn't put a seatbelt on, stretched one arm over her handbag. A soft silence drowned her. Cosied by the weather and the smoothness of the car, she let her head fall back against the seat and felt the lazy powerlessness ahead of her. I suppose I'll be there in ten minutes, she thought, and then, I wish we could drive for hours. I wish I could glide along, on my way, forever.

She heard other traffic, voices, even the meow of a cat, but she didn't move her head to look outside. The tops of buildings went by. They were in a more residential part of town now, moving more slowly.

Then there seemed to be no noise at all. Annie listened hard and heard the engine, quiet, and the creak of a pedal under the driver's foot. She sniffed, softly, just to check that it made a noise too. And then another sound, the driver singing to himself, as if there was no one else there, as if he was shaving or polishing his shoes. A song that she didn't recognise was tiptoeing out from his throat. She turned her head to the right, noticed they were on another busy, wide road, going faster again, gathering speed.

"Are we not in town yet?" she said, leaning forward. The driver's singing stopped, but he didn't talk.

"Aren't we in town yet?" she asked again, moving forward on the seat, raising her voice a bit and looking through the windscreen to the heavy sky. The driver smelled of salt and maybe beer. He wore a blue T-shirt tucked into faded jeans, with old grey trainers that were so battered and squidgy they were basically slippers. His cheekbones and his pointy little nose did not match the heft of him – he was big, American, tall. He slouched back in his seat, one hand loosely on the bottom of the steering wheel and the other in his lap. He was too tall to spend his days in this small car.

"This is the way," he said, and his eyes didn't even flick up to the rearview mirror.

"Sure," she said, and sounded like an Englishwoman using an American word.

"The I-10's a mess today."

He was talking as if she knew the city's roads, and she liked it. Perhaps he was lying though.

"A mess?"

"Construction work by the park."

She said nothing, moved back. She was so clearly a tourist, and he was so clearly in charge. Why worry?

The car turned into a smaller street, then onto another main road. Annie felt they were going back north, which would be the wrong way. The quiet singing had started again, and she still couldn't hear the song but she enjoyed it anyway. It was slow and deep and pleasing. The backseat felt even slippier, she slid down a little further and across, left or right whenever the car moved to the right or the left. The idea that she was being abducted by a violent criminal flooded quietly into her brain, and she sank into it. The worst-case scenario really was that he was taking her a longer route in order to charge a higher fare. She shook her head a little and asked, "How much will it cost, the trip?"

"You're okay," he said.

"What?"

"Forty dollars, forty-five."

Well that's okay, she thought, seems fair. And a tip, of course, and I'm enjoying this ride through the city, smelling the warm wet air, even if you kill me and throw me in the Mississippi.

But nothing like that happened. They even had company, for a while: the taxi stopped at a junction while a procession of tiny dogs all linked together made their way across, led by a little girl, and a trumpet player stood on the pavement, music exploding from him while his friend, sitting on the ground, clapped along now and again and laughed. She tried to give them the two dollars change she had in her wallet, but the taxi pulled away as she was getting it so she just gave the trumpet man a smile. He didn't see her.

And then they were at the guesthouse, a big clapboard place set back off the main road with wooden steps leading up to a porch. She recognised the owners, Fred and Elaine, from the smiley picture they had on their website. They were sitting out with glasses of beer.

"Annie?" said Fred.

"Hi!"

"Welcome," said Elaine, coming down the steps with arms spread. Annie stepped over to the back of the car, rather than into Elaine's open arms, to get her bags. The driver was still in his seat but he'd unlocked the boot so Annie took her things and carried them towards the front steps, all the while smiling at Elaine and saying "that's fine" and "no thank you, don't worry at all," but then Fred was there too, hands out, and so Annie gave up and handed him her things. She went to pay the driver. His window was open and she wanted to lean in, her arms on the frame, cock her head to one side, chat to him. But she handed him the notes instead, three twenties, and was glad not to have to wait for change.

"That's yours," she told him. "Thank you."

She walked with Elaine up the steps, past the table with two beers and an ashtray. Fred was already at the door, just inside, and he waved Annie towards a second open door, just inside the hallway and to the right.

"Here's your room," he said, proudly. "One of our favourites."

There was curvy mahogany furniture, stinking lilies on the side table, a view over the street through long muslin curtains.

There was a chaise longue, no less, scrolls on the bedposts, a marble mantelpiece, a ceiling fan and a heavy door leading to a white-tiled bathroom. Fred and Elaine offered her coffee or a beer – "no, thank you" – and left her alone.

Annie stood at the window and looked out at the street, which was almost empty, because it was mid-afternoon and baking out there. At the small grassy patch just across the street, oak trees gave shade to a tiny old man and his slow, barrel-bellied dog. She let her attention glide around outside her window, content to be close to the centre of things, and then slowly turned back into the room, took a shower, brushed her teeth, put on a fresh dress and stepped out into the city.

She walked right down Burgundy and then zigged back up and around towards the top of Frenchmen Street. A little way down was a corner restaurant, decorated in black and white, with smart young men in suits waiting tables. Annie took a chair by the window, a few feet in from the open door, and smiled a hello to the staff.

She held the menu in front of her, but her gaze was up and into the street. It was a wide view, north and east, three or four blocks each way. The sunlight had gotten pearly; it made all the different faces and voices – pretty and squealing children, sweating and gruff men, chubby and fragrant ladies – part of the same soft scene. There was no music in the restaurant, so she could hear the syrupy bounce of the voices inside and outside, a conversation between two people strolling along the pavement, a shout ("Hey sweetie!") across the street, the man who owned the bookshop on the next corner ("Four dollars each. Six for the both").

She ordered, feeling very English – a cup of tea and a cheese toastie. Close by she heard low, lazy voices; the sound of young, lazy men. A group of boys sat at the table across the room, past the door and in front of the other window; they looked about twenty-five, although one was maybe a year or two younger.

He was especially beautiful. His face was soft and calm, ringed with curls. He had dark eyes and a big mouth. He watched his friends with an open, serene expression. Annie saw how different he was to his three companions. They sat forward, knees apart, feet flat, and they wore identical T-shirts, jeans, trainers. Their short hair framed vacant, doughy faces. The boy glowed next to them. His hair was not cropped: it curled right over his ears and at the top of his neck. His seersucker jacket – pale blue and white, unbuttoned over a pink shirt – made him look old-fashioned and a bit silly. He sat half-facing Annie, with his legs tucked under the chair, sandals on his tanned feet, and one arm across the back of a friend's chair. He reclined, watching the other three, an observer like her. He had that look of someone who gets ill a lot. Sickly. Or was he just delicate, precarious? Beauty is alive, thought Annie, a dizzying concert of flukes and nearly-nots, and it is always about to leave.

She watched them as she ate, occasionally looking at something else but always finding her attention back on the beautiful boy. Then one of the other boys said something Annie didn't quite hear, and the four of them began to rustle and reach for phones and jackets, money for their bill. They had an appointment, a plan for the evening, but they were languid too and not quite ready to go anywhere. Annie leaned back, watching them, watching the boy.

Then one of them stood, and another, and they were on their way out of the door. The beautiful boy pushed his chair back and waited while the others went ahead of him. He looked sleepy and noble. As he reached the door he slowed and looked round the cafe. He scanned across to her and she realised that she was looking straight back, her mouth a little bit open, her eyes wide open, as if he was a picture on a screen and could not see her. He did see her though.

There was nothing exceptional about any of this. The young men had eaten, talked, paid and left. The most beautiful of them had moved a little slower, that was all. But it had all seemed so deliberate, with such concern for space and shape and colours, with the light falling just right on his face and hair and clothes. Annie waited for a few minutes, paid her bill, and walked out through that same door into the sweet damp evening.

She got a drink – a margarita, like a tourist – in a small, busy bar down the street, and settled in to watch the crowd. Three women were at the next table, talking about a film they'd seen.

"Nothing happened, really, and still it was so good," the tallest, thinnest one was saying. They were all elegant, a bit younger than Annie maybe, drinking long drinks.

Then the tall one turned to Annie. "Cute dress," she said.

Annie smiled in thanks.

"Cute pumps!" said her mate, with curly red hair.

"Get me," laughed Annie. "Aren't I cute?"

"Oh my gawd!" the tall woman said. "Cute ACC-ent!"

Annie was in their gang after that, just for the next couple of hours. They discussed school ("We're postgrads"), assessed men walking past ("Fuck, he's hot"), and got one, two, three rounds of drinks in. Annie was included in the rounds straight away, which seemed oddly British to her, and she got a shimmer of homesickness.

It turned out the three friends were staying in an apartment a couple of streets west of Annie's guesthouse. Before they called it a night, though, they went to a second bar a few blocks over in Marigny, taking go-cups with them. ("What kind of a city has go-cups?" said Annie, delighted, then answered herself. "My kind of city!")

Waiting to get served there, leaning on the bar, Annie sang along to the jukebox.

"Heaven must have sent you-ou, into my aa-aa-arms."

And the man standing next to her, with a big moustache like Captain Pugwash, sang along, "Oooh-ooh-ooh."

Annie grinned, because he was tall and handsome and singing oooh-ooh-ooh to her, looking at her with his big moony eyes.

"Shall we dance?" he said, and held out his hand. They danced right there, to the rest of the song, and it was clumsy and nice. Every so often she did a little spin while he held her hand up in the air. And when the song ended he gave her a kiss right on the mouth, almost chivalrous but not quite. She stood on tiptoes and leaned into him, like a chaste-ish maiden, then put one hand against the small of his back and pulled him against her for more kissing. Right in the middle of the bar, drunk.

Then she looked over to the three friends, who were watching and grinning. They cheered when she saw them, then the tall woman said, "Where in the hell are our drinks?", with her arms outstretched like she was singing a showtune.

Annie rested her fingertips on the moustache man's chest for a couple of seconds, looked at the buttons on his blue shirt, then turned back to the bar for those drinks.

"Ah, baby," he said, softly, and went to get his drink too. When she and the others headed to their beds an hour or so later, she nodded and smiled to wish him goodnight on her way out the door.

*

It was muggy the next morning, the air slow and grey under a slow grey sky. Annie slid open the window and damp air fell into her lungs.

She headed out for a walk – to buy a dress, maybe, or a coffee, or just to explore the streets and the parks and the river, have a sugary beignet, buy a souvenir. There was some life in the Marigny and the French Quarter and along the river, a few strolling people with things to do but not in a hurry. Annie looked down at her feet, one two, one two, and her hands, and she wiggled her fingers. Under her skin there seemed to be a thin layer of lead. She was not sure if she was inhaling properly, whether air was actually going into her, and supposed that she'd find out soon enough.

And then, instead of walking to a shop or a park, she just went back towards the guesthouse. The air seemed foul, poisonous. Everything was covered in grease and dust. She felt bullied by the other people in the streets. Her palms were sweaty and she felt a distant rage. She lay quietly on the bed and thought about leaving the city. She realised – and it was more an observation than a decision – that she would have to go. Why stay? There were other places she could visit in the US. She had friends in New York, and San Francisco.

She didn't say goodbye to Fred and Elaine. She had cash to leave for them, and she wrote a quick note – apologies-goodbye-thank-you – then packed her bag and walked out the door. She hadn't booked a flight; she would just get the next one available. She walked down the street, hot, lugging her bag, then stopped on the corner and waited. A taxi came so she hailed it, got in, half expected her burly, surly driver again. Instead it was a short, fat woman with quick movements and a constant smile.

Five minutes later they were on the I-10 when Annie said, "Sorry, sorry, I'm sorry."

The driver's smile fell just slightly.

"I changed my mind," said Annie, and it was happening at the same time that she was saying it. "Can we head back into town? I don't know where to yet."

The driver's smile was reignited. And why would the driver care anyway, even if that was odd behaviour? Annie had wanted to leave and then she did not. She had changed her mind again. Which was, in fact, like never having changed her mind at all. She would go on wanting what she'd wanted that morning – the dress, the coffee, exploring the new city. It could easily have been ridiculous and embarrassing, to decide to leave and then to whizz right back so soon, and wasting money on a taxi too. But there was no one to tell.

It began to rain, heavily. Warm drops hit the car windows like crackling electricity, water streamed down the road. Annie wondered if Fred and Elaine had already seen her note, and decided to just go to another hotel. There was an old-fashioned place she'd seen near the French Quarter with dark wood panels and hanging plants, tiled floors, brass lights. Annie headed there. She'd be able to get grits for breakfast and stay up late drinking hard liquor at the bar.

Her room was on the second floor, overlooking the dampening street. She sat by the window, with a long glass of iced water, watching. It got dark and she watched. That night she slept a deep and happy sleep, hours of bright dreams and slow wriggling on clean sheets.

*

As Annie strolled down to the French Quarter the next morning she walked into a sweet nugget of the world so good she almost cried. Four children wheeled past on bicycles, streamers flying from the handlebars, their wet little mouths squealing. At the beignet place tourists sat alongside local families and workers in suits, all with powdered sugar and paper napkins and cups of coffee. A long row of market stalls was a strip of energetic exchange and interrupted saunter, sales and chatter, bags passed over piles of oranges and bananas, change dropped and recovered or forgotten. Further away by the river people promenaded in shorts and vests, in pretty dresses. On the right, a band of teenagers played trombone and violin and drums; others sat or stood around, watching, dancing, clapping. On the left, on Jackson Square, a family had spread themselves on the grass – men with beards and smiles; slender women, clean and efficient; an older woman, maybe a grandma or an aunt, with a paperback and a shawl; two fat babies; a little boy playing with a bottle of water. They were cheery, having fun, shouting jokes and sharing food, putting on silly voices to make each other laugh, kissing and hugging, squeezing and nuzzling.

I'll stay in New Orleans, thought Annie. Why would I leave? She sat on a bench, leaned right back as if to widen her view and thought of the Mississippi rolling just out of sight. She loved the water and for all kinds of reasons: the bathing and the cleaning, the desire to be drenched and submerged, the crushing blankness, the soft dark weight. She imagined herself paddling in the river, then gliding just under its surface, part of the flow of it, a city mermaid. Her mind relaxed into the smooth wet daydream for only a few seconds before something tickled her gaze. The beautiful boy walked into view, in front of the coffee shop. He stayed a little way ahead of his friends, who chatted just behind him. He had bare feet and cut-off shorts but didn't seem affected or scrappy in his Huckleberry Finn-ness. He looked over to the square and saw the family, and he smiled at the babies. They were the first thing Annie had noticed prompting a response from him.

A kind of nervousness, something like modesty, made Annie's eyes drop to the floor just as it seemed the boy might look at her. She prickled, felt bleak, adolescent, embarrassed. But she was giddy too, at the thought of him walking past and perhaps noticing her, though probably not, but walking past anyway with his dirty feet, his soft joints, his long fingers and curly hair.

She looked at her hands, kept her head still, and listened to the boy's voice, a high and wavering voice, as he responded to his friends. They were buying coffees and "Nah, thanks," he didn't want one. But then, "Actually, yeah, I do," he said. "And a beignet."

"One more, for Jerry," one of the others said. And that was his name, then. She wasn't sure she liked it.

"Just plain, black, whatever, no sugar," Jerry said. Jerry. Plain, black, whatever, no sugar.

She liked the sound of Jerry, maybe. A bit too much like a pet's name, but that didn't seem so bad. And she liked the way he said 'beignet', with a slightly embarrassed flourish.

Sitting there in the shade, she took yesterday's newspaper from her bag, settled in further, began to read. After not even one minute, though, she decided it was a waste to look at anything other than the beautiful boy, when the beautiful boy was so nearby, and she looked up and around hoping he hadn't gone already.

There he was, sitting on a low wall with his friends, facing her across the street and the marketplace. They had pastries and coffees in their hands, and they leaned one way and the next, heads tilting in time, as if they were singing but she couldn't hear any song. Four of them, in shorts and T-shirts, having fun and looking so much like toddlers that she was surprised their feet could touch the ground. One boy, with blond hair, seemed to be Jerry's closest friend, seemed to look at him a little more, smile when Jerry spoke. As the four eventually walked away, off stage-right, Jerry walked ahead again but then the blond-haired friend closed in behind, put his hands on Jerry's shoulders and pushed himself into the air before falling back to the side of Jerry, wobbling into him, and the two began to chat, almost in confidence, and walk side-by-side.

Annie was charmed and jealous. She turned back to her reading for a few seconds, but then walked over to the market and got a bag of peaches. It was a hot day now, a day with nothing to do. Her mind began to feel grey and dull, even as her mouth was filled with sweet sharp fruit goo. Annie thought about Jerry, and walked over to where he'd been sitting. She rested there, in his spot, and pleasure welled up in her.

She started to plan the rest of her day. She would browse the city, investigate the streets, eat lunch, buy a dress, find a little park. Then, as she sat there, Jerry and his friends headed back towards her. Surely they would notice her, surely Jerry would notice that the two of them were in the same place yet again. But he did not. Beautiful boys, she thought, don't look around them as much as everyone else does. And then she realised that his legs were bony, that his eyes had dark circles and his fingers were actually a bit grubby. He is puny and filthy too, she thought, and felt consoled.

*

From then on, day in and day out, the sun shone hard, slow and steady. The heat was barely ever ruffled by the sticky soft air. Faces glistened and shimmered. Soft crumbling walls and tendrilled plants provided shade and good smells while Annie sat and ate breakfast, drank tea, drifted along on the hours. The evenings were balmy, of course, and fragrant, of course, with drinks and dancing and good food, and strolls along the riverside. Travelling alone, it is easy to go for days without really speaking to anyone, just a few hellos and pleases and thank yous, sometimes a neighbourly chat with a stranger at the bar, friendships in miniature and gentle flirtations, although no more old-fashioned dancing with big moustachioed men.

Then a few days after she booked into her new hotel, sitting at her bedroom window and watching the street, something wonderful happened. There was Jerry, outside, with his friends, and they walked up and into the lobby. This was where they were staying. It was as if she'd known, and Annie almost panicked that she had known, that she'd followed him, but it wasn't true. This was a real coincidence. She smiled. Beautiful Jerry, so close. She listened to see if they were on her floor, in the same corridor as her, but she didn't hear a thing from inside the building, just chatter outside and the rain softly falling.

She did not think about flights again. In the new hotel she unpacked everything, tidied her cases out of sight, with her passport tucked away inside them. She steadily filled the drawers and wardrobe to brimming with silky clothes she bought in secondhand shops and cutesy boutiques. She got familiar with a few cafes and a couple of good restaurants, and got to be more than a tourist in the hotel bar. She drank sazeracs, nearly always, and watched and listened, and sometimes chatted to the bartender – a young, cherub-cheeked woman – about books or music or wine or a pair of new shoes (bright purple) which Annie had bought that day and which skidded a little on the hotel's floor but which looked strange and fabulous and were therefore – they agreed, while the bartender made another sazerac – worth the risk, the danger, the potential banana-skin slapstick comedy of it, even (probably) enhanced by it.

Annie was bewitched by this easy life, so brilliant and simple and busy. "Busy doing nothing," she'd sometimes sing to herself. What a place this is, with so much nothing to do. A small city and a great drifting river. Annie was pleased by everything.

Her skin felt the touch of clothes and moisture and air, and the occasional glances of people around her. She did not want excitement, exactly, she wanted a routine packed with pleasure. Over and over and over again. There were times, when she sat at the bar, or walked the dark avenues, or looked over the water, or read at an outside table, or watched a band play in the street, when she remembered London and felt guilty to have left her flat and her job and her friends. But she liked it better here. The days flowed past.

Annie saw the beautiful boy, Jerry, most days, not just because they were staying in the same hotel but because they naturally seemed to be in the same places: he'd be sitting in the lobby with his friends when she walked out one evening, she'd pass a shop window and notice him inside, they would have lunch a few tables apart in the same restaurant – Annie would be paying her bill as he arrived, or vice versa.

Most often she saw him on his way somewhere as she sat in Jackson Square or on that low wall. She'd settle into a spot late morning and stay there for two or three hours with a book or a magazine, although she often didn't read a word. And he would walk past. She expected that one day he wouldn't appear, but he always did. Maybe he was on a long, long holiday too. Sometimes he would look her way and smile, say hello. Sometimes she would smile back. An almost daily occurrence, a delicate coincidence that strung one day to the next.

Soon she recognised his physical habits: the angle of his head when he was listening, the lope of his walk. How he would half-hug a friend when they met. How when he was sitting he would rest a foot across his knee and run a finger back and forth along his shin. How sometimes, in his group of friends, he would step back from them very slightly and stare at the wider scene, at old men walking by, or their pet dogs, or the sun setting beyond the bridge or a boat going past. Annie enjoyed everything about him. Half-formed thoughts swelled and stretched inside her, thoughts that had long been flattened by language and properness. Time alone in the warmth can elate your sleepy soul. So decided Annie, and smiled.

The boy walked across the square one morning while she was sitting on a bench by the gate. She could smell the air, full of sugar and fruit and damp. She put her hands flat on her legs, pushed down hard, felt the cloth of her skirt under her palms, on top of her thighs. The dazzle of the light, she thought, and every moment of your life. She laughed, then stopped, wondering if she had made any noise, or too much noise.

That same evening, while she was sitting at the hotel bar, Jerry and his friends came in and sat at a table by the front window. Annie noticed the bartender look towards them and inhale, as if she wanted to breathe them in. She caught Annie's eye, and told her that they'd been staying at the hotel for a few weeks, were due to be here a few weeks more. Studying, she said. Sweet guys. From Idaho, maybe, or Wyoming.

Annie hadn't said a word, hadn't revealed a syllable of desire, and this information had popped out, unasked for and excellent. She would stay too. For a while. She'd had no thought of leaving, really. The money trickled into her bank account, topping up her savings, and she could rent her flat out for more if she needed to. These facts would waft in, and she saw them clearly, dealt with them, never worried. It was admin and she'd had years of admin. Floppy little grey puzzles to solve, and she solved them. It didn't take long anymore. What took time was feeling the smooth firmness of the bar, the sticky glow of the lights, the pretty refractions through all the liquor bottles, the freckles on the bartender's cheeks and nose, the bursts and silences of the traffic outside.

Annie rested her chin on her hand, looked down at her shallow brown drink, looked across at herself in the mirror, then turned slightly as Jerry and his friends were getting up to leave the hotel. There is something delicate and strange about two people who don't know each other but who see each other so often. There was a quiet esteem, Annie felt it. She watched, or half-watched, as Jerry and his friends gathered up to go and she didn't feel creepy or awkward. He was so beautiful that she sang stupid soppy songs in her head.

The others hadn't noticed her, but Jerry quite unexpectedly looked right at Annie as he walked out of the bar. Relaxed, in a slow stride, he smiled at her with an unabashed, me-and-you smile. It was a smile that offered everything, besotted and beguiling. He walked right past and Annie turned back to the bar, shocked silly. A few minutes later, the beautiful boy came back into the lobby without his friends. The bartender looked at Annie, smiled, raised her eyebrows.

"You want a drink?" the bartender asked him. God love her.

"Mmm, gimme a beer. Thanks."

He gave Annie a polite nod, as if he was arriving at a job interview, then sat on the stool next to her.

"I'm Annie," she said. She'd straightened her back and sat with her elbows on the bar and one hand dangling towards her sazerac. Classic sexy-older-woman-at-a-bar pose, she thought. Maybe.

"Jerry," he said, and smiled a gentler version of that lobby smile. "Where you from?"

"London," she said. "Well, not originally."

"I love London. I went there for three months one summer. Got shitfaced, saw lots of art." He said 'shitfaced' in a Dick Van Dyke voice, enjoying himself, and said 'art' with a hoity-toity comedy flair.

"Two of the very best things to do in London."

"What brings you here?"

"Holiday. A break."

"Nice. This is such a great city. I don't want to leave. We've been here a few weeks, and it's time to head back home soon. Which'll be just awful."

He laughed, because it wouldn't be awful really, and took a swig of his beer. Annie looked at his neck while he drank, looked down to his easy posture, felt a bit giddy and had another sip of her drink.

They talked about music, because the bartender was playing The Kinks ("another fucking great English band," Jerry said, as if they'd just released their first album). They talked about the weather and it wasn't even boring. They talked about The Country Club and The Decatur Lounge and some places she didn't know in the Garden District. He listened and enthused and seemed to look at her in very much the same way that she was looking at him.

"Another drink?" she said, when he'd finished his beer. "What would you like?"

"I'd like to go to bed with you," he said. He looked either terrified or excited, she couldn't tell. Annie glanced at the bartender, who showed no sign of having heard.

He leaned towards her, inhaled softly, and actually bit his bottom lip as he smiled at her. For a moment she thought about the fact that she might, for all he knew, say no. Then she asked the bartender if she could take her glass upstairs.

"Sure thing, Annie," she said, with a wink.

His room was on the same floor as hers, but he had a view out the back, and twin beds – he was sharing with the blond boy – instead of her grand double. A bottle of whiskey sat on the side, next to the tiny fridge. It wasn't a complete mess, but it wasn't tidy either. Shoes, pants, unmade beds. Tangles of headphones and phone chargers, a few books (she noticed two Kurt Vonnegut paperbacks, felt pleased and then laughed out loud at herself for feeling pleased).

There was a sofa, as well as the two beds, and that's where she sat while he poured drinks – whiskey on ice. Huge whiskeys. Then he knelt down in front of her, his hands on her thighs, and she leaned down to kiss his beer-and-whiskey lips. He pulled down her top and pushed up her skirt and kissed her, and he looked extremely happy.

"Ha!" he said. "I need to make sure I slow down a bit." He laughed again and kissed her, very gently and with his hands pulling down her pants. She felt great.

And for a while she barely moved, barely did anything at all really. She just wanted to watch him and enjoy. She wanted that good solid obliterating fuck. Then they spent an hour or two, playing and fucking, and then they dozed off, and then she went back to her own room before his friend got home and walked in on them.

*

Sitting at the end of her own bed, looking out the window early the next morning, Annie watched the still, blue sky. The stars disappeared into the dawn. Everything might in fact be about to collapse, she realised. Chaos may actually ensue. Messy horror.

She found it tricky to think of anything other than Jerry. The heat and the wet and the promise of flood all seemed to be in his service. That day she read, a little bit, and ate at the cafe with the beanburgers and the wheatgrass smoothies; she visited the art gallery and went out for fancy dinner. Going back to her room that night, she stopped outside his hotel room, stood almost pushed up against it, drunk and careless and wanting to eat him.

She did wonder whether she was a silly fool who needed to get a grip. Silly fool, she'd think, get a grip. It was someone else's voice though and she didn't listen. She thought of her mum, and her grandmas, and aunties, and great-aunties, and women drinking and smoking and dyeing their hair, badly, and wearing good coats and shoes and lipstick and having a good time. She thought about the boy's body.

Even when he wasn't there, she felt like she was watching him. She let possibilities loom from the corner, and she didn't turn to face them.

The next evening, after she'd eaten a hot fishy soup in a bar around the corner, Annie got back to the hotel and found there was a band setting up in the courtyard through the back of the lobby. It was the woman and the men she'd seen busking in the street a few times, and they were dolled up – silky dresses, shirts and ties – and sitting on the hotel's fancy chairs, sipping from the hotel's fancy glasses. Guests surrounded them, some sitting and some standing with drinks in hand, waiting to indulge the local show. Hotel staff – the bartender, the man from reception, a waiter, a cook – leaned in the doorway or against the wall, ready to be back at work at any moment. And Jerry was there, with his friends. They were sitting on comfy chairs, great upholstered armchairs, which they must have carried outside from the lobby. How well did they know the staff here? They sat, they slouched, limp and warm.

Annie perched on a chair by an iron balustrade. The trumpet trumpeted and the singer sang and Annie relaxed. The band played louder and louder, and Annie watched Jerry smiling. He leaned forward, his elbows on his knees, and then he looked right round, over his shoulder, straight at Annie. He saw her, in her chair, leaning back against the railing, one arm draped over her head like a ballerina toy, and he mimicked her pose. It made her laugh, just a little, and he laughed back too, in just the same way. Other times, when he had caught her eye, his friends had called him over, taken his attention. This time they did not notice, they were watching the band, and the boy looked at her for another second or two before slowly dipping his head and looking back up towards the music. Annie looked at him, the back of him, thought of how he would die too, shrink away, and she felt a satisfying sadness, an excitement at the thought of him ripening and then rotting.

Most of the guests left and the staff got back to work, but Annie stayed to finish her big glass of pink wine and Jerry lingered in his armchair after his friends had gone. The evening arrived; time was melting. There had been a lamp on her mum's desk, when Annie was a child, a bronze miniature, a naked woman with her arms held out at her sides as if she was preparing to dive into deep water. All at once Annie could see it again, see the tiny woman's poise, see the light snap on, the gleam on the bronze, the about-to-go-ness of it.

When Jerry walked past she smiled at him, said hello, and he looked so relieved, so eager, like a sweet dog. They went upstairs, to her room this time and her big double bed. They drank more whiskey and talked, and talked about sex and had sex and then lay hot on the bed for a while, and then had more sex – hard, happy, nuzzling, grabbing sex, more of it. Then they showered and they smooched a bit, and then they headed out.

It was Saturday night and they went to the bar on Frenchmen where they had both been, when they hadn't yet spoken, the previous Saturday, and maybe the Saturday before that. There was live music, the saggy-faced man with the saggy voice sang, and the bartender made huge margaritas. Annie sat at the bar and watched him. Jerry's friends were at a table nearby, and they all said hello and smiled, one even waved to her. She didn't talk to them, though, and they didn't talk to her either. The city seemed to be getting sadder, more scared, it did not look like so much fun.

"Is this fun?" she asked the woman sitting next to her. The woman laughed, and then leaned forward and kissed Annie on the cheek.

She could see Jerry reflected in the mirror behind the bar. She imagined herself going home, back to London, and her face screwed up like a pantomime dame sucking a lemon.

"I'm staying here," she said and smiled at the kissing woman. The bar was full and hot, and people were dancing in pairs as well as in groups, jiving but doing it badly because they were young and didn't know how to do proper dancing. Doing it badly but looking so good too, getting it all wrong. The clamour, the stamping and swinging, the racket, the din, the hubbub, the twisting and spinning and the sweat, the holding hands. Drinks wobbled and spilled.

Jerry was right next to her, one hand on her waist and one hand on the bar. She imagined the others all washed away, so that it was the two of them, with him just so beautiful. There was a fantastic logic, a certainty, the sort you feel in a dream or after you've stumbled headlong into the right dose of music and tequila. She didn't really want to hear his voice. He said something but it was too quiet, underneath the music. He caught her eye in the mirror and smiled, then leaned in so his nose almost touched her neck. She smiled too and leaned back towards him. Then his friend, the boy with the blond hair, pushed through to help with the drinks and Annie said she fancied an early night. "Ah, okay," he said, surprised but still sweet and smiley. She kissed him, just a peck and a squeeze, slipped down carefully from her barstool, bobbed through the dancing crowd and let the night air dry her sweaty skin on the way home.

*

Annie came down late the next day, after lunch, because she'd eaten poached eggs on toast and drunk tea, lots of tea, in her room and watched trashy television and enjoyed her hangover. Across the street and over towards the murky Mississippi, Jerry and his friends were playing on the patch of grass in the park, dashing and yelping like little boys. She walked over, felt like she'd arrived at the cinema just as the film was starting. There was an empty bench, so she sat down and waved hello to Jerry and the others. They were wrestling, tumbling around, and the blond one got Jerry in a headlock. He had Jerry face down, straddled him, tickled him, but Jerry was shouting, he didn't like it. The blond boy swung off him, as if he was getting off a horse, and Jerry jumped up. He was sulking, like a child! Annie watched, almost laughing, smitten.

Jerry had walked off, ignoring the shouts – "Jerry! Sorry Jerry! Sorry sorry Jerry, so sorry!" – of his friend. It was hot and he looked tired. He would be going back home soon. She watched him, one hand on his hip, wearing his shorts and his pink shirt, aloof, alone, so pretty, looking out at the grey water and looking down a little. All at once, as if she'd poked him, he turned right round and looked at her. He turned softly like the little doll in a child's jewellery box and gave her a beautiful smile. The fuzzy sun was behind him, and the arm that was on his hip lifted like a helium balloon, as if he was beckoning her over. She didn't move so he came to her, floating really, and when he got close enough that she could see the tangle of his eyelashes and the soft tip of his tongue, she stood up.

"Let's go back to bed," she said, and he smiled, and they did.

*

That evening, as it was starting to get dark, Annie went for a walk by the river. She went past the market, past the railway lines, past the bridge, past empty yards and car parks, flowerbeds and water fountains, down to where the houses got scrappier and there were fewer people around. She walked to the edge of the Mississippi, where the water lapped on silty ground, and barely paused. The great grey river reached her knees, then her waist, soft and not as cold as she'd expected. The water squeezed her ever so gently, lifted her ever so slightly. It was dusk, a little beyond dusk, and the lights on the opposite shore twinkled and shimmered. Annie stumbled a bit on the pebbles with her arms raised, like a tightrope walker, because she wanted to get further in, closer to the opposite shore. As the water reached her chest her arms were lifted anyway, floating on the soft surface. She looked at the grey ripples, felt herself tall beneath them, felt that twinkle and shimmer from the other side, felt herself getting lighter, rising. If anyone yells, she decided, I won't even turn round, I'll ignore them and keep going.

Meeting

I remember how, alone on the front step, I waited so long that I forgot I'd ever knocked on the door and I just stood there, rather enjoying myself, the sun warming one side of my face, pink-purple flowers on a trellis to admire and a damp crumbling section of doorframe to investigate. I gazed, already fond, at the brass knocker and almost reached up to stroke the shiniest part of it. Then the door opened and there I was: another me, looking at me, not older or younger, just another me, warm and happy to see me. So comforting. "Ah," she said. "Come on through."

And I remember we took a chair each in the parlour, at a dark wooden table with shallow drawers underneath full of bits of paper and elastic bands and a box of matches, a stubby pencil.

A shuffly pretty young man sat down beside us, looking miserable. We didn't mind or care.

"So tired," he told us. "I'm so tired. Can you help me?"

I felt perhaps that I actually should try to help him, but I didn't want to. Other Me agreed. And what could we do anyway?

"I feel bitter," he told us. "And I feel shame." He sighed. "Shame and bitterness."

I looked at Other Me, and then we both looked at him, at his pale arms and bony wrists, at the pores around his nose, greasy, at his long eyelashes. He smelled like washing powder and cigarettes.

A young woman came in, chucked a glance of solid disdain at the young man, and sat right down at the table. Four of us. Two of me, and two of them. The young woman was beautiful; young people are so beautiful. She had been crying and now she was biting her lip and huffing a lot.

"Nothing brings me joy," she said, a propos of fuck-knows-what. The young man nodded. I didn't want to know what they were talking about, and neither did Other Me. I put my hands on the table, like a woman with a ouija board, and began to wiggle my fingers. I wiggled my toes too, reminiscing already about the quiet time I'd enjoyed on that warm doorstep.

Other Me saw that I was zoning out, bored. "Be not afear'd," she said, and winked. "We'll go next door, it's sunnier in there." I liked having her in charge.

I could already smell vanilla-scented cake from the next room and felt no doubt there'd be paper doilies and friendliness. Not quite puppies and pink roses and brown paper packages tied up with string, but also not far off. We left the grumpus pair to it, went through to the lounge.

My friend Janey was in there with her three children, chatting and listening, and they didn't seem at all surprised to see two of me. Her children were each so different and all so similar to Janey, like three bright colours on a flag or a turning tree. The youngest ran over, to both of me, for hugs. A chatterbox, a smiler. Mandy was in the sunnier room too, and she was indeed putting paper doilies onto the coffee table, and then Midwinter plates, and then eclairs, chocolate eclairs. Dear beloved Frank was having a nap in the corner. Proust, more or less, went through to the kitchen to make tea.

"We're going to sit here and talk for a little while," Other Me told me. "Then I'll have to go out the front door, and you'll head out the back."

"Okay," I said.

"Nobody will know I'm not you," she said. "After all, I am you."

And then Other Me told me about the back garden, and what I'd find out there. Soft sweet air, she said, and the walls pulsed gently. Rain on greenest leaves, mossy earth underfoot, a nice cup of tea, if I want one, the cuddliest cat and a pond for paddling. All days of glory, joy and happiness.

"What do you think of that, dear pal?" she said. And I loved it.

♥

Andy Morwood, Eugene Noone, Catriona Ward, Alice Slater, Buku Sarkar, Hannah Harper, Nell Pach, Debra Isaac, Emma Healey, Jenny Karlsson. Sharlene Teo, Shelley Oria, Aja Gabel, Katie Bellas.

Andrew Cowan, Henry Sutton, Michèle Roberts, Stephen Benson, Jean McNeil, Zoe Fairbairns, Tessa Hadley, Giles Foden, Jacqui Seddon, Mike Hinken, Philip Langeskov, Blake Morrison. Marion Gow. Mickela Sonola. Wendy Erskine. Jenny Lord. Matthew Turner at Rogers, Coleridge & White. Susie Nicklin at The Indigo Press. Sam Jordison and Eloise Millar at Galley Beggar Press.

Janet Green, Beverley Oliver, Beth Evans, Nicky Haynes, Joanne Orgill, Sarah Urmson, Mr Howard, Mrs Harris.

Ingrid Kopp, Yung Kha, Maxyne Franklin, Susannah Zeff, Ellie Hutchinson, Kate Aubrey-Johnson, Zoe Coleman, Lucy Atkinson, Thilini Gunaratna, Jacqui Chanarin, Chrystal Genesis, Emma Deeks, Nitasha Kapoor, Esther Bryan, Sophie Brown, Shanida Scotland, Katie Green, Jacqui Rice, Lori, Sophie Dening, Anna Lobbenberg.

Zoe Miller, Jenny Bulley, Danny Ecclestone, Pat Gilbert, Ted Kessler, Matt Turner, Chris Catchpole. Mandy Wigby, Kath McDermott, Helen Keegan, Jeff Barrett, Adelle Stripe, Lisa Cradduck, Jackie Thompson, Diva Harris, Patrick Clarke, Andrew Walsh, Una Thorleifsdottir, Mandy Rowson.

Maxi Marshall, John Marshall. Jackie Kay, Carol Ann Duffy, Denise Else, Ella Duffy, Flo Carr. Rachel Wood. Julie Pemberton, Ida Scott. Barry Wood and Tricia Wood.